Average

KINGS OF THE EAST #14

CHARITY PARKERSON

PUNK & SISSY PUBLICATIONS

Copyright

—Warning: This book is intended for readers over the age of 18. Some of my books contain allusions to past abuse and trauma. I try to have nothing triggering on page and treat every situation with care.

Copyright © 2023 Charity Parkerson

Editor: BZ Hercules & Consultants

CHARITY PARKERSON

Cover art: Morningstar Ashley | Designs by Morningstar

Contents

Introduction

JERICHO WANTS NOTHING MORE than a normal life. Edward is as average as they come. Too bad things are never that simple.

As one of Zander's team leaders, Jericho's hard work is finally paying off. When he moved to the east coast to run the first cleanup crew on this side of the country, he stayed too busy to date. Plus, with a past like his, he's not really relationship material. Now new teams are pouring in, and Jericho has all the free time to focus on his social life and the man he's been eyeing for months from a distance, Edward. He can't explain why, but he's convinced Edward will accept everything about him. Maybe so, except Zander has a new plan for him that could upend all of that.

Edward didn't know Jericho existed until two weeks ago. If he had, the gay panic would've been real because Edward is as plain and as boring as they come. He's a librarian who gave up on love a long time ago. There's no way someone who looks like Jericho is truly interested in him. Edward doesn't mind having a new friend, though. He just wishes Jericho didn't make his heart beat quite so fast. Oh, boy. He's in trouble. More than he even realizes, especially when he learns what Jericho really does for a living.

AVERAGE

Average is the fourteenth book in Charity Parkerson's Kings of the East series where assassins, crime lords, and mafia bosses run the world. These books are best when read in order.

Author Note

THIS SERIES IS DARKER than my usual writing. If you need a list of potential triggers, you can skip to the end of this book and find a list after the About Author page. You can also visit my website at charityparkerson.com/kings-of -the-east, if you'd prefer.

Chapter One

THERE WAS A SMALL tea shop near a bookstore in a neighborhood within walking distance of Edward's home. The place smelled like cinnamon, and—until two weeks ago—no one ever bothered him there. Edward would take a book, order tea and a chocolate croissant, and savor his Fridays alone. Maybe it was a crazy way to spend his day off, since he was a librarian and worked with books all day, but it felt like heaven to him. Edward lived a quiet, unassuming life, and always kept to himself. It was his biggest misfortune that he had been born gay, since he wasn't especially handsome or brave. It was a death sentence for any sort of love life. But books existed and Edward had thought he had accepted his fate of living inside them. Once again, until two weeks ago.

Like any other Friday afternoon, Edward had been sitting in his favorite spot inside the tea shop. He had been lost in the world of supernatural fantasy when a man with heart-stoppingly beautiful blue eyes had set a book at his elbow, capturing his attention.

"Hang on to this for me, will you? I'd like to chat next time I come in." He had winked and kept moving without waiting for a response, as if he had known Edward would do exactly as he asked. He had

been right. Edward had been back each Friday with the book in tow, expecting the stranger's return while trying not to look too desperate. That was a tall order for someone who hadn't had anything that exciting happen to him in literal years.

Last Friday had passed and Edward had been disappointed but not surprised when the man hadn't returned. Today, he almost hadn't brought the book along, but he couldn't leave it behind. Edward told himself the librarian inside him couldn't have an overdue book in his possession. Lying to himself was his favorite pastime after reading. He arrived at exactly two in the afternoon—the way he always did—only to find his favorite table already occupied. All he saw was the back of a dark head before he moved along. Edward headed toward a different table. A hand shot out, stopping him before he made it past. Edward glanced over to find his beautiful stranger seated in his spot.

"Oh. Hi." Heat climbed Edward's cheeks as he listened to his ridiculous greeting. He had been caught off guard. That was his only excuse.

"Hello."

Wow. He was... wow. Edward startled when he realized he silently stared like an imbecile. "Oh, yeah. I have your book." He set it on the table. "I don't know why you left it with me, though. I mean, I am a librarian. But surely, you can't tell that just by looking at me, right? Oh, God. You probably can tell that by just looking at me, can't you?"

The sexy stranger smiled. He doubled in sexiness. It was unfair. "I'm Jericho.

AVERAGE

Please, sit down. I left my book with you because I've been looking for a reason to talk to you for a while, but something always seems to get in the way. Just like that day. I was headed to speak with you when I got called away to work."

Edward sat. He was too stunned to keep standing. "I'm Edward. Nice to meet you. Why would you want to talk to me?"

Jericho looked from side to side. While wearing an adorable grin, he lowered his voice. "This is the gayborhood tea shop."

Edward blinked. "I'm aware."

Jericho shook his head, but his smile never wavered. "You like to read."

Now they were on familiar ground. A smile snapped to Edward's lips. "Yes. A little too much, probably. It's all I do." His smile slipped. As he heard himself make that confession to such a gorgeous man, he wondered how pathetic he sounded. He cleared his throat. "When you left your book with me, you said you wanted to chat with me. Did you have a question about the story? It's been years since I read this one, but I remember bits and pieces of it."

"I haven't read it yet."

A laugh burst from Edward. Nervousness ran with his tongue. "Yeah. I guess it would be kind of hard since I've had it. Like I said, I remember bits and pieces. I also kind of remember something about the author being somewhat problematic. That's why I never finished the series."

"Why were they problematic?"

AVERAGE

Edward swore he felt himself falling into Jericho's light blue eyes. He couldn't recall the last time he had this good of a conversation with anyone where someone seemed to genuinely listen to his every word. It made him forget his every thought. Edward forgot to be shy. "You know, I don't really recall. It's been a few years."

Jericho smiled, making Edward want to sigh. "I'll grab us some tea and croissants. While I'm gone, you can choose a different book for me, since you're obviously the expert." He stood. "Earl Grey and the chocolate croissants, right?"

Edward blinked. "Um… Yes." He had no clue how Jericho knew that.

"Good." Jericho pulled out his phone and clicked around before handing the device to Edward. "Just one-click whichever book you choose for me, and we can sit and read together. I don't mind reading on my phone. Honestly, that's usually how I read my ebooks is from the app. The dark background is less straining on my eyes."

Edward accepted the device. "Are you sure? Most people don't like reading together. Won't you get bored?"

Jericho's face screwed up in confusion. He was still ridiculously hot. "Why? I like to read, and I enjoy your company. It sounds like an amazing way to spend an afternoon."

Edward fought a blush. It was ridiculous for him to read too much into Jericho's claim. There was zero chance Jericho wanted anything more than friendship. Jericho was an eleven while Edward was a three on a good day. They did not match. Still, he liked the idea of having a friend. "Okay."

Jericho nodded and started away before changing course and returning. "Oh, and while you're clicking around on my phone, add your number, okay?"

"Okay." Edward had no clue why he kept agreeing to everything Jericho said, but he didn't think it was possible to say no to the guy. Not with Jericho looking directly at him with those amazing eyes. The devil's eyes. Edward shook his head as Jericho walked away. This was one friend zone that was about to hurt like a motherfucker. Yet Edward couldn't think of anywhere he would rather be.

His face hurt from smiling. Edward was every bit as nice as Jericho expected he would be. Jericho felt like he had waited ages to meet the guy. He had been coming to The Tea Box for months, watching Edward read alone. Jericho had tried to keep up with the books he read to start a conversation that way, but Edward read too fast. Before Jericho could start the last book he saw Edward reading, he was already reading something new. Unfortunately, Jericho didn't have that much free time. Leading the first biohazard team to the east coast for Zander meant very little time off until more guys relocated or were trained. Finally, teams had recently started pouring in, and Jericho had time to focus on himself. He had one personal goal, winning a quiet mouse named Edward.

A few months back, he had been headed inside the bookstore when Edward had been headed out. They had collided when Edward had stumbled forward. Edward's books had gone flying. Jericho had tried to help Edward pick up the mess, their heads had bumped, and then their gazes had met. For him, it had been like something out of a movie. The sunlight had hit Edward's brown eyes, making their amber hues pop. Edward had blushed and stammered his apologies. Jericho had been incapable of saying a word. Edward had moved along, and Jericho had followed at a safe distance to here. He hadn't stopped coming back since or watching Edward from afar. What he had learned was a bit sad and not all that different from Jericho's current existence, truth be told. Edward worked and came here with the occasional side trip to the grocery store or doctor. He just lived a regular, boring... lonely life. That was all Jericho wanted, except for that last part. Jericho was tired of being alone, but the quiet thing, he fucking needed that. He needed all that shit for the rest of his entire goddamn life. Anyone who had been trafficked as a child, as he had been, would feel the same. Jericho just needed a normal life now. Edward felt very peaceful to him. The last thing Edward needed to worry about was Jericho getting bored while sitting and reading with him. That was all Jericho wanted in life.

With their order placed, Jericho returned to their table. "They'll have our order out shortly."

Edward smiled. "Great. How much do I owe you?"

"Nothing. You can pay next time." The way Edward smiled made the offer worthwhile. It felt like things were going well. He hadn't been sure if Edward would be interested in him since Edward had practically run in the opposite direction the day they had collided outside the bookstore. Jericho had learned the hard way over the years that normal people didn't enjoy spending time with fucked-up people like him. They might like the way he looked. People might enjoy fucking him. No one wanted to keep someone with a past like his. He was damaged. That wasn't for everyone.

"Oh," Edward said, as if recalling he had Jericho's phone. He passed the device back to Jericho. "I wasn't sure what your favorite genre is, so I just picked one of my favorites for you. It's something magical."

His smile made it hard for Jericho to look away, but he forced himself to eye his app. "What's this one about?"

"It's all things paranormal, really. There are vampires, shifters, and even a merman. You'll see."

The excitement in Edward's voice couldn't be missed. Their order arrived, and they settled in to read. Silence filled their tiny booth. Several times, their feet brushed beneath the table. Their gazes met each time. After a smile passed between them, they would return to their books. Despite himself, Jericho was engrossed by page one. In no time, he went along for a magical ride on a hunt for demons. He laughed aloud a few times. Edward made a good choice.

"I'm sorry. It's just occurred to me I know next to nothing about you. What do you do for a living?"

At the question, Jericho tore himself away from his book and focused on Edward. "I'm a biohazard specialist. I clean up crime scenes."

"Really?" Edward sounded fascinated. "I'd ask if you have any good stories, but I read somewhere crime clean-up crews are right up there with EMTs as far as PTSD goes."

He had no idea. Jericho had PTSD and lots of other letters too. "You should let me make you dinner tomorrow night and you can ask me whatever you'd like then."

Edward didn't hesitate. "I'd love to, but I work on Saturdays. That's our busiest day at the library."

Jericho knew from following Edward; he didn't work that late. "What time do you get off?"

"Seven."

"That's not too late for me."

A smile snapped to Edward's lips. "Good. Great. Sounds good. I added my number to your phone. Just text me your address and I'll come by as soon as I get off work."

Even to Jericho, his smile felt wicked. Edward was as good as his already. He just didn't know it yet.

Chapter Two

EVERYTHING LOOKED BRIGHTER. EDWARD smiled so hard all day his cheeks hurt. He swore he weighed less. More than he cared to admit, Edward hid in the back corner of the romance section where no one could find him just so he could daydream all day. He wasn't dumb. Tonight wasn't a date. Oddly, Edward was every bit as happy to have made a friend as he would be if he'd met a man. His life had been sadly lacking for a while. Last night had been... nice. He still couldn't believe how easily he had talked to Jericho. It had been like he had known the guy for years. He was never like that with anyone. Edward was notoriously shy and awkward. He thought it might be Jericho. Jericho was just nice, and he had kind eyes. He made Edward feel so damn comfortable in his own skin. Maybe the guy had an old soul or something. Whatever the reason, Edward was giddy as hell about seeing him again.

"Why do I keep finding you hiding back here?"

Edward startled when Sandy rounded the corner. He fought to squelch his smile without luck. "Sorry. I guess I'm having some weird weekend fever or something."

Sandy eyed him. "Did you get lucky last night or something?"

AVERAGE

Edward rolled his eyes, but his smile came back without his permission.

Sandy gasped. "Oh my god. You did."

"Shhh." Edward glanced around, making sure no one heard. Sandy had hired him seven years ago, and they had been friends ever since. They were too free with each other sometimes. "I didn't. You know I would've texted you something like that."

Sandy's tiny frame somehow got smaller as her shoulders fell. "Oh."

Edward chewed his bottom lip. He immediately felt guilty—like he kept something from her. "I did make a new friend, though."

Her green eyes lit. "Oooh. Do tell. Is he handsome?" She gasped. "Is it the mysterious guy from the tea shop? The one who left you the book?"

"Yep." Edward felt dumb for blushing, but it had been such a nice night. No one had made him feel so good in years. Edward wanted to bask in it. "He's so nice." The words burst from Edward before he could stop them. "He bought me tea and croissants, and we talked about books. It turns out he was coming to my table to talk to me when he got called away to work and that's why he asked me to hang on to his book, so he wouldn't miss me next time. He's making me dinner tonight."

"This sounds like more than a friend."

Edward shook his head. "You wouldn't say that if you saw him. He's beautiful."

Sandy rolled her eyes. "Why would you say that? You're adorable. He'd be crazy not to want you."

Edward shrugged. "It doesn't matter. I'm still over the moon. Sorry if I've been useless today."

She waved off his apology. "To hell with that. We have a different job to do. Let's go." Sandy took the books from his hand and set them aside before dragging him down the aisle.

"Where are we going?"

"We're taking our lunch break. Tina can handle things for an hour. We have to rev up those Scorpio vibes. Bring you into your power so you can take down that hottie tonight."

A laugh burst from Edward. "My Scorpio what? What are you talking about?"

"Blacks and reds. Form fitting clothes. You've got this. We have to get you a new outfit. You can't walk in there tonight without at least trying." Sandy stopped and met his stare. "Look me in the eye and tell me you can live with knowing you didn't at least try to win this man."

He couldn't. God help him. It would haunt him if he didn't try.

With a sharp nod, Sandy got moving again. "Then let's go. We only have an hour lunchbreak to get you ready to take his breath."

Edward had a bad feeling this was a hopeless endeavor. He was uncomfortable just thinking about trying to seduce anyone, but Sandy was right. He had to try. Plus, what could a new outfit hurt? He hadn't bought anything new in ages. It was just clothes. Everyone needed new clothes eventually. Edward wouldn't overthink things. God help him. He was fucked.

By the time Edward's knock came, Jericho's nerves were a complete mess. He hadn't had or been on any sort of date in years. At least, not one he hadn't been paid to be on. He had always known how those would end. With Edward, Jericho wasn't so sure. Jericho might end up totally crushed. He hadn't thought to ask what Edward liked to eat. Jericho hadn't considered how much he would panic. Now Edward was at the door, nothing was ready, and Jericho was a mess. He opened the door more frazzled than he liked.

"Hey." He nearly swallowed his tongue. Draped from head to toe in black, Edward looked hot as hell. There was just a hint of red in his form fitting shirt and it was only enough to bring out the amber in his eyes. Jericho liked it. "Are you a Scorpio?"

A loud laugh burst from Edward, taking the knots from Jericho's shoulders. "As it happens, I am."

Jericho couldn't stop smiling. "I can tell. You look amazing. Come in." He took a step back so Edward could pass. "Sorry, but our food isn't ready yet. It occurred to me way too late that I didn't know what you like, then I decided to go with pizza from scratch, because everyone likes pizza, right? But then, by then, it was already almost time for you to be here and the dough needed time to rise and... I'm rambling," Jericho concluded when Edward merely stared at him wearing a bemused expression. Jericho took a breath. "Would you like a tour while the oven is warming?"

"Sure." Edward toed off his shoes by the door.

Jericho took a breath and offered his arm to Edward. Edward accepted, and Jericho motioned toward the room behind him. "The living room." It was pretty bland and bare, but cozy. He had a small TV and a huge comfy couch. Most of the walls were covered in various bookshelves, with books stacked haphazardly in every direction. There was no filing system. He read a book and stuck it on the shelf before moving on to a new one. That was it. Jericho headed through the mouth of the hallway. "Here's the kitchen and dining room." Again, it was nothing special. Serviceable appliances and a table with two chairs. Jericho moved down the hall. He motioned toward each door as they passed. "Bathroom, home gym, catch-all room, and finally, my bedroom with another bathroom. That's about it. Feel free to make yourself at home."

"You have a lot of things in boxes. Are you moving soon?" Edward asked as they headed back to the kitchen.

"Actually, I recently moved here from California. Well, not like recently, recently. Like almost two years ago now, but I've been crazy busy. Things have just now started to slow down enough for me to unpack a few things."

"Really? Which part of California?" Thankfully, Edward didn't sound put off by the fact that Jericho was a mess who lived out of boxes.

"San Francisco, mostly." Jericho didn't know how to explain he didn't really have a permanent address before moving to Cage Beach.

Thankfully, Edward didn't find fault in his answer. Edward eyed the explosion of unchopped and uncooked food. "Would you like some help? If we double team this, it won't take as long."

"Sure. That sounds good." Jericho was back to feeling somewhat nervous. Something about the night didn't feel very date-like and he had a bad feeling that was a failing on his end. He glanced around. "Um. If you want to slice the pepperoni, I'll work on getting this crust ready to go."

"Damn. You even have real unsliced pepperoni. That sounds like a task I'm up to."

With a place to start, Jericho led Edward to the counter and found a cutting board and knife for him. They washed their hands and moved around each other to work on dinner. Edward sliced the pepperoni. Jericho stole a chance to watch him. He truly was adorable. Normally, he dressed like he didn't have a care in the world. Tonight, it was obvious he had made an effort. That gave Jericho some hope he was interested. Obviously, Jericho wanted him no matter what, but Edward trying meant he might be thinking more about Jericho in a certain way. Damn, he was really overthinking this and he couldn't stop.

Jericho decided to press his luck a hair before he drove himself insane. He crowded Edward's space, reaching past him for the rolling pin. With his hand on Edward's waist, Jericho pressed against Edward's back and spoke close to his ear. "Excuse me."

A sharp gasp cut through the air. Edward jerked away and dropped the knife. Blood dripped on to the counter.

Without thinking, Jericho whipped his shirt up and over his head and used it to wrap Edward's hand. He kept pressure on Edward's fingers. "Don't panic. I've got you."

Edward looked completely unfazed. "Were you just looking for a reason to take off your shirt?"

Jericho blinked at Edward's calm tone.

"There's a roll of paper towels right there. I'm really not even that hurt."

Jericho blushed and dipped his head to hide it. "Sorry. I saw blood, and I panicked."

Edward's gaze moved over Jericho's chest. "I honestly couldn't have guessed your shirt hid so many tattoos. You're..." he cleared his throat, sounding uncomfortable, "... impressive. No wonder you were in such a hurry to take off your shirt. I might not ever put one on if I looked like you."

Jericho's ears felt hot. Things weren't going as planned. "I've got a first aid kit in the bedroom. Come with me." He held tightly to Edward's hand, in case the cut was worse than Edward let on. He didn't think he had overreacted. There had been a lot of blood. Maybe a paper towel would've been better, though.

His phone rang as he pulled the first aid kit from beneath the bathroom sink inside his bedroom. Jericho bit back a sigh and pulled on a pair of surgical gloves. "Keep pressure on that. It's my boss. I have to take this." Jericho answered Zander's call while he opened a fresh pack of gauze and disinfectant. "Hello?"

"Hey, Jericho. It's Zander. I'd like to do a face-to-face."

"Tonight?"

"If possible."

Jericho unwrapped the t-shirt from Edward's hand. There was a slice across his forefinger. It bled freely, without pressure. Jericho swiped it with the gauze and then the disinfectant. "I'm on a date right now. Can it wait until tomorrow?"

"Yes. I have some free time in the morning, but it'll have to be early. I'll have the jet waiting for you at six."

Even though Zander couldn't see him, and the phone was held between his shoulder and ear, Jericho nodded. "I can do that."

"Okay. I'll see you tomorrow. Enjoy your evening."

"You too." Jericho disconnected the call while keeping his gaze locked on the cut. "This is deep. I'll have to glue this closed unless you'd like me to take you to get stitches."

"Glue is fine. You called this a date."

Jericho glanced up from his task at Edward's observation. "Yeah. Is it not?"

Edward looked pale. Truthfully, he looked like he might faint at any moment. "Honestly? I didn't think so, no."

"Oh." Jericho didn't know what else to say. He wasn't surprised. Not really. He always carried this irrational fear people could see his black soul from a mile away and knew he was a lost cause. Tonight proved he was right to feel that way. His chest hurt. An invisible weight sat on his shoulders. Edward was right not to want him, but Jericho was still disappointed. Jericho glued the wound. He blew on it until the glue was completely dry. Then he covered it with a bandage, all while trying not to meet Edward's stare. He didn't want Edward to see his disappointment. Edward had still shown up tonight. Surely that meant something. Yet Jericho fought the urge to ask Edward to leave. He wanted to be alone with his pain.

"I don't fantasize about meeting people," Edward said, as if just picking a place to start his confession. Jericho found his gaze moving toward Edward's face at the sadness in Edward's voice. A small smile touched his lips before falling away again, fascinating Jericho. He shrugged. "It's impossible for me to picture anyone seducing me because I'm not the least bit sexy in any way." Edward took a ragged-sounding breath that let Jericho know he had never said these words to anyone before now, so Jericho listened despite his complete disagreement. "At some point, I just gave up to wait for death, I guess. I get my adventure and romance from books and binge-watching shows. Then I go to bed and go to work, and I try not to catch my eye in the mirror too often. I damn sure don't let myself stay awake with my own thoughts for too long." Edward shrugged again. "It doesn't make sense for someone like you to want someone like me."

It was obvious he felt exposed. That was the only reason Jericho didn't argue. Edward was entitled to have his feelings. Jericho decided to expose himself so Edward could see himself through Jericho's eyes.

"I was trafficked as a child."

Edward gasped.

Jericho flashed him a sad smile. He let go of Edward's hand, in case Edward didn't want to touch him anymore after learning that truth. Lots of people treated him as if he was dirty. "I was actually specifically bred to be sold. Dark hair and light blue eyes are a particular taste to a certain clientele. They'll pay a lot of money for that combination. I was kept until I was sixteen, which is much longer than most children, but the man who bought me as a baby was unusually attached to me." No amount of therapy made exposing himself easier, but Edward had been honest about himself. Jericho would be too. "Still, I did eventually get too old for him. He gave me twenty grand and dropped me in the street in San Francisco. From there, I ended up working as a prostitute for a while until an organization that saves trafficked children scooped me up and helped settle me into my current career." Jericho tried and failed to smile. He closed the lid on his first aid kit. "I try not to catch my eye in the mirror too often either. There's nothing about me I want to look at too closely. You're nice, Edward." Jericho met Edward's stare. "I find that extremely sexy in a man. I don't think you realize how few people in the world are genuinely good. But if you didn't want this to be a date, that's okay. I get it. I'm not a catch. I wouldn't choose me, if I were you, so you can say that to me. I mean, I'll be disappointed but—"

"No. I want this to be a date," Edward said quickly, interrupting him. He immediately blushed. "I think you're nice too," he said a little slower, as if trying not to sound too enthusiastic. His hand landed on Jericho's bare chest.

Jericho's heart sped. He hadn't expected Edward to willingly touch him after his confession. "Can I ask you a personal question?"

Edward nodded.

"Do you go by Edward?"

A sexy chuckle fell from Edward's lips and Jericho knew he would never hear the answer, because he had never wanted to taste a sound so badly in his life. He touched his lips to Edward's. For a moment, neither of them moved. Then Edward shuffled closer, and Jericho's lips parted. He held Edward's bottom lip between his. Each move they made came slowly, as if they equally feared scaring the other. Then they moved at the same time. Their tongues met and stroked. Edward was in his arms, and Jericho didn't recall moving. It was over almost as quickly as it began. They held each other's stare and struggled for air.

"I still want to make you dinner."

Edward nodded. "I probably ruined the pepperoni."

"I have more."

Neither of them moved.

"Everyone calls me Edward, but you can call me whatever you'd like."

Jericho nodded. "I guess I should find a shirt."

Edward licked his lips, looking nervous. "You don't have to, if you don't want to." He stroked Jericho's chest. "I'd love a chance to get a closer look at these tattoos. I'm not sexualizing you, or anything."

A smile exploded across Jericho's face. He genuinely liked Edward. "It's okay if you want to sexualize me a little. I'm sexualizing you in these jeans."

"Really?" The hopefulness in Edward's voice had Jericho scratching his head.

"How do you not know how adorable you are? That's fascinating."

Edward blushed and bit his bottom lip.

Jericho took a step back before Edward felt the way that look stirred him. Tonight, they would eat pizza and talk. Maybe they would kiss again. But Jericho wouldn't press for more because he wanted this for real. Apparently, he had to be in California in the morning, but when he got home, he would see Edward again. Edward had shown him affection. It was over for him now.

Chapter Three

THE FIRST TIME JERICHO had been brought to the home of the Kapra, he had been twenty and jaded as fuck. He had been standing on the street corner, strung out and probably not much longer for the world. Jericho had long passed the point of caring if he lived. Hell, maybe he never had. Life had never offered him a single comfort. Then a black SUV had picked him up and brought him here.

The humongous estate had both impressed and intimidated him. He hadn't known if he had been rescued or just enslaved under a new name. Sometimes, he still didn't know. While no one forced Jericho to his knees anymore, he also wasn't free, but he was clean. While he could quit his job and go work as a barista on the beach somewhere, he actually couldn't. Because Jericho knew what really went on behind closed doors in every town, and he couldn't stop trying to end it. It was dumb, really. He didn't think they were even making a dent in the underworld of sex trade, but those monsters knew they weren't free or safe to travel through the docks. Jericho had helped make that happen. That meant something to him. The people under this roof meant something to him. He couldn't walk away from this life. Likely, he would die in servitude to the cause. Days like today made what he wanted with Edward feel like an impossible dream. He very much doubted sweet Edward would ever accept this.

"Hey. You made it."

Jericho turned in his seat as Zander stepped inside his office. To his surprise, instead of his usual bodyguards, Pytor and Yaro, Zander had his husband, Maverick, with him. Jericho smiled at the pair. "Hey. Yeah. Everything went fine, as usual." Jericho's gaze moved to Maverick. It had been a while since he had seen Zander's husband. Maverick fought the MMA circuit and Jericho didn't make it out to California as much as he used to. He had always liked Maverick. While he moved like a predator, ready to strike, his honey-colored eyes were kind and they always watched Zander with some unnamed emotion Jericho wished to have for himself. Not with Maverick, obviously. Maverick wasn't his type. "Hey, Maverick. It's been a while."

Maverick nodded. "It has been. How's the east coast treating you?" The couple didn't move to sit behind the desk. Instead, they moved to the opposite side of the office where a couch and loveseat sat. They cuddled together on the loveseat.

Jericho answered Maverick's question as he moved to the couch. It was obvious they intended this to be an informal meeting. "Honestly, it's great."

"He's met a very sweet librarian," Zander interjected, proving—as always—there wasn't much that slipped by him.

Jericho's smile grew. "I have. Things are still in the first stages, but I'm hopeful."

Maverick eyed him. "Huh. A librarian. I guess you did always have a book with you when you lived here."

A snort escaped Jericho before he could call it back. He always found it funny the things people remembered about him. If Maverick wanted to remember him always having a book and not his hunt for an escape from the withdrawals from a horrible drug addiction, then whatever. "I still do that."

Maverick nodded as he squeezed Zander closer to his side.

Zander rubbed Maverick's leg. A blond hair fell across one light blue eye and Zander tucked it behind his ear again. He looked unusually unkempt today, as if he had rolled out of bed for this meeting. "I've been doing some self-reflecting since the whole Wulf and Beau thing."

Jericho nodded. It didn't surprise him to hear Zander was still haunted by that. Jericho's team member, Wulf, had fallen in love with his now-husband Beau. When Zander had investigated Beau, he had discovered a sealed juvenile file. After having it unsealed, he had learned Beau had served two years in a juvenile facility for rape. Unfortunately, it wasn't until after Zander ruined Wulf and Beau's relationship, they had learned Beau had been the one who had been groomed and Beau had tried taking his own life because of Zander's interference. Everything had worked out in the end, but it had been a near miss. Jericho waited to hear why Zander brought up the incident again now.

Maverick squeezed Zander's shoulders again, as if lending him strength. A small smile touched Zander's lips and he continued. "When we expanded to the east coast, obviously, it was with the best intentions. We have to cover as many ports as possible or these bastards will just find a new place to do the same amount of business. We have to squeeze them. But here, I have eyes and ears everywhere. I know what's going on. Here, I genuinely feel like I'm keeping my people safe. That's my number one priority." Zander held Jericho's stare, as if he needed Jericho to see the earnestness in his eyes. "I never want a single person I save to feel victimized again. Not by the system and certainly not by me."

"You're not God." Jericho felt moved to speak. He knew Zander probably felt infallible, but no one was, not even the great Kapra. "You can't see into the heart of every man. Beau might've been a bad person."

"But he isn't, and I might've known that, if I had time to look into him before lashing out, but I didn't and I don't. The number of lives it would've destroyed if he had died is inexcusable. Nothing I can do will repair the seed of mistrust I've sown."

Jericho didn't know how to respond to that. He didn't know if Zander looked for an answer. People had always come to Jericho with their problems. He had never known why, so he just listened. That was all he had to offer, so he gave it.

A kind smile touched Zander's lips. He looked more human in that moment than he ever had. "What did you think of Beau? When you first met him, I mean."

Jericho shrugged, feeling uncomfortable and put on the spot. "It doesn't matter what I thought."

"It does. Please humor me."

Jericho blew out a sigh. "I thought, Wulf loved him and that was all that mattered because Wulf is a grown man who can take care of himself if things didn't work out."

A low rumble of laughter came deep from Zander's chest. His eyes swam with humor. "Very diplomatic, but you didn't answer my question. What did you *think* of Beau?"

Jericho gave in. "Fine. I thought he was a head case, but so is Wulf, and so they're really fucking perfect for each other. I figured one day they'd end up exactly as they are now, happily married as one crazy couple, living a completely normal life, far away from this mess that was destroying them."

Zander's humor didn't dampen at Jericho's opinion dump. "Thank you for your honesty. That's exactly why I want you to take over the east coast."

"What?" It could have been a whisper or a shriek. Jericho couldn't hear himself any longer to judge. He scrambled to stop whatever was happening from happening. "The east coast belongs to the Alexeyev. I'm not trying to get myself killed by the Italian mafia. Like I get that I work for you, but you can't ask this of me."

AVERAGE

"Xiv Alexeyev runs a legitimate business now and I'm not talking about setting up shop anyhow. I have my casinos here and you know we get a fuck ton of income from seizing the trafficking accounts. You're the person everyone comes to when they have a problem. I need you to be me but there. I can't be on both coasts. But I also can't let things happen like I did with Beau because I can't live with that. I'm supposed to be making survivors' lives better. All I'm asking is—"

"Everything," Jericho said, cutting in before Zander fed him some bullshit. "You're asking me for everything. If I say yes, I'm you for the rest of my life. That's no small thing, Zander."

"It's not," Maverick said, speaking up for the first time. "And you're allowed to say no. We would never expect you to give up everything without some real time to think about this. We know what we're asking."

Did they? Jericho wasn't sure he even understood the full depth.

Zander made a calming gesture and spoke softly, as if he expected Jericho would explode any second. "You're so much like me. It's insane, really. People trust you. For good reason. You're a good person and I know you'd be an amazing fit for the position. I'd let you build your own team, of course, since they'd likely live with you. This is huge, I know. Please take your time. Think it over and call whenever or however many times you need to talk. This is a huge promotion, but I also get that it's a major change to your life. I wouldn't have asked if I hadn't considered every man I know for the job and decided you're the strongest candidate. You're the one people trust."

Jericho was flattered, but there a was voice screaming in his head for him to say no. Yet he didn't. He couldn't. Not yet, because Beau had almost died from what Zander couldn't see. Jericho didn't blame Zander. Zander had been trying to protect his people, but if he had asked Jericho, Jericho could have told him Beau was harmless. Zander was spread too thin. Jericho's mind wandered to Edward as his gaze moved to the couple sitting across from him. Would Edward accept him the way Maverick accepted Zander? If Jericho was being honest with himself, he had been moving toward getting out. Wulf had gotten out and Dante had recently made some noises like he didn't feel the same about the job either since Wulf left. Jericho thought maybe he saw the light at the end of the tunnel, even though he hadn't known what else he would do with his life. Now he knew that light was a train, and he didn't know if he would ever get to have a single dream that was his. He had never felt this lost or alone. Jericho wanted Edward.

Water carried suds down Edward's body and down the drain. A ringing cut through the air. He froze. The sound came again. Edward stuck his head outside the shower curtain. His cellphone rang in the other room. Edward jumped from the shower and dashed from the bathroom, soaking the carpet while barely clinging to his towel to get to his ringing phone. "Hello?"

"Why are you out of breath?"

Edward tried harder to sound like he wasn't dying. "I was in the shower."

"Oh. Call me back when you're done."

"No. I'm done." Edward winced at the desperation in his voice. No doubt Jericho would tire of him quickly with the way Edward was obviously hard up for his attention. "I mean, I was finished. We can talk. How's California?"

"Stressful. Are you still nude?"

Heat flooded Edward's face. He didn't get a chance to think of a response.

"Ignore that. I don't want you to think I'm only after one thing."

Edward was flabbergasted. "I didn't think that and yeah. I am." Wow. Was that his voice? He sounded sultry. Like he wanted Jericho. He did, but whoa. He hadn't known he had it in him.

Jericho took an audible breath. "Damn. I really wish I wasn't on the opposite side of the country right now."

"Me too." Edward sat on the bed, uncaring of his nudity and still wet body. He was engrossed by Jericho. "Why are you stressed?"

"I got offered a promotion."

A smile snapped to Edward's lips. "That's amazing. They flew you there for that? It must be huge."

"Mhmm. It is pretty life-altering."

AVERAGE

"You don't sound happy."

Silence met Edward's observation. For a moment, he didn't think Jericho would speak. Then Jericho cleared his throat. "I'm just not sure what I want yet. It's a lot of money and I wouldn't have to travel any longer."

Edward bit his bottom lip. He liked the idea of Jericho staying in Cage Beach, but it wasn't his decision to make. "I hear a 'but' coming."

A sexy chuckle caressed Edward's ear, making his eyes fall closed. "But it's very different from what I do now. No more field work, and if I hate it, too bad. I have to sign a very long and ironclad contract since I'll basically be the guy in charge of the east coast branch of the company."

"Wow. That's... wow. They must really think highly of you. Just tell me how I can help. Do you want me to talk you into it or out of it? I'm here for you either way."

Jericho took another audible breath. "I want you to tell me what you did when you got home last night."

Edward bit his bottom lip and sprawled out on the bed. He stared at the ceiling, losing himself in the moment. "I came through the door, stood in the middle of my living room, and stared into space for like twenty minutes while trying to decide if you were for real."

"What did you decide?"

"That I don't care," Edward answered honestly. "I've never wanted anyone as badly, so I'm willing to risk that life is playing a joke on me."

"You confuse me."

Edward didn't want that. "How so?"

"I don't understand how I can be so…" Jericho blew out an aggravated-sounding breath as if he couldn't find the right word. He started again. "I don't know how I can feel so alive and happy and turned on every second I'm with you and you just don't see it for whatever reason. You're all I think about."

Edward bit his bottom lip again. The backs of his eyes burned. Happiness had him overwhelmed. He had to take a breath before he could respond. "You're all I think about too."

"See me again when I get back in town."

As if Edward could say no. "Okay."

"Then see me again after that."

"Okay." Edward couldn't stop smiling.

"Be my boyfriend."

Edward covered his eyes. "Okay."

"Are you still nude?"

"Yes." Damn. He was in over his head, and he couldn't stop.

"Describe your room to me."

Edward looked around. It never occurred to him to say no. "As you walk in the door, the closet is to the right and my bed is to the left. There are oak nightstands on either side of my bed."

"What color is your comforter?"

"Black with red flowers."

"Mhmm," Jericho hummed, as if he could picture it. Edward's body stirred at the sound. He swore he felt it against his skin. "Which nightstand has your toys?"

Heat flooded Edward's face. He fought the urge to claim he didn't own toys. Years of religious shaming was hard to shake. "The one closest to the closet."

"Good. That's need-to-know information. Are you a top or a bottom, Edward?"

Fuck. Something about Jericho saying his name while asking that question had Edward's cock getting even harder. "I'm a bottom."

A ragged-sounding breath came through the line, as if Jericho touched himself.

Edward's eyes fell closed. His hand slid down his body. He strained to hear any hint he might be right.

"What about you?"

A wicked-sounding chuckle caressed his ear as Edward's fingers encircled his erection. He bit back a moan. "I'm everything, Edward. I'll top, bottom, suck, eat, or whatever it takes to make you writhe."

Edward stroked, needing relief with Jericho's sexy voice in his ear. "That's not what I asked. I asked, what about you? What do you like? What do you want?"

"The answer is still the same. I haven't stopped fantasizing about having you since the day I literally collided with you outside the bookstore. I didn't catch your name that day, but I knew I would catch you. Now you're mine and I want everything with you. You should come for me, Edward."

Jericho kept saying his name. Edward's mind was a mess. Until Jericho said the words, he hadn't remembered that day outside the bookstore, but he had literally collided with Jericho several months back. They had nearly run each other over as Edward had been coming out of the bookstore and Jericho had been going inside. Edward's books had gone flying. Then they had bumped heads as they had tried to pick up the books at the same time. He had been so mortified by the situation, since Jericho had been so incredibly hot, and Edward had been every bit as awkward as always, he had run away and put the incident out of his mind. But that had been Jericho and now Jericho claimed to have wanted him ever since. Edward's dick sawed in and out of his hand. He was on the edge of orgasm, and nothing looked clear. Edward felt more powerful and sexier in that moment than he ever had in his life. Jericho's heavy breaths drove him. With his eyes closed, it was like Jericho was there.

A whimper came from the back of Edward's throat. He couldn't stop it.

"That's it, beautiful. I want to hear you come. When I get back, I want to see it. Fuck. I can hear how fast you're beating your dick. That shit has me so hot. I wish you were sitting on my lap. You have no idea the things I could do to your body."

The pressure nearly drove him insane. It climbed and built. Edward dug his heels into the mattress and fucked his hand. He whimpered and cried out as he crawled closer to the edge.

Jericho moaned. "God I can't wait to fuck you."

AVERAGE

Edward blew. A gasp tore from his throat. Cum hit his stomach. He stared down the line of his body and watched the cum coat his skin. The sound of his harsh breathing caressed the phone and Edward felt no shame because Jericho sounded the same.

"Goddamn. I'm ready to get home to you."

How had they just met? Edward had never wanted anything to work out as much.

"When will you be here?" Edward couldn't believe how needy he sounded yet he couldn't take it back.

"Tomorrow. I'll come to you as soon as my plane lands."

"I have to work." As much as Edward hated that he wasn't independently wealthy so he could be free to see Jericho the second his plane landed, he couldn't change his schedule. Fridays and Sundays were his only days off.

"I'll still be there."

Edward believed. He had faith. "Okay. I'll be waiting."

"Go finish your shower."

A laugh burst from Edward. "Okay. I'll see you tomorrow."

"Yes. You will." With that, Jericho disconnected their call and Edward stared at the ceiling. Tomorrow couldn't get here fast enough. Edward was already addicted.

Chapter Four

IN THE BACK CORNER of the romance section, Edward found himself—once again—daydreaming about Jericho and avoiding work. In his defense, Edward never really took any time off work and nothing this amazing had ever happened to him. It was like spring fever and puppy love all wrapped in one. The darker the sky turned and the closer it got to him going home, the worse Edward's anxiety spiked. He swore his skin crawled like electricity zapped through him. His feet moved closer toward the door and his gaze moved toward the clock. Sandy hadn't asked him about his date yet, but they had been too busy all day to talk. With the library closed on Sundays, Mondays were a nightmare. She headed his way. A smiled snapped to his lips. She already knew. There was no way she didn't. He was too happy and he couldn't hide it.

"Bitch," she whispered, drawing out the word as she reached his side. "You'd better tell me every detail."

The door opened, bringing in the unusual fog that had settled over the city. Their gazes moved that way. Jericho stepped through the door draped from head to toe in black. His eerie light blue gaze swept the room before landing on Edward.

AVERAGE

A breathless-sounding sigh escaped Edward before he could stop it from happening. He didn't even need to tell Sandy this was the one. There was no hiding his reaction. His entire soul sang at just the sight of Jericho.

Sandy gasped as Jericho headed their way. "Holy shit. He's a Scorpio too. You lucky bastard."

Fuck. Edward didn't have time to consider where he was or his boss standing next to him. Jericho was there, and he overcame Edward like they hadn't seen each other in years. He bit Edward's bottom lip and Edward swore he almost came.

"Okay. Well, I'm okay with you cutting out a few minutes early this one time."

Edward pulled away because he had to hang on to some good sense. "Um. Wow.

Sorry. I guess I missed you a little. You should meet my boss and also my friend Sandy."

For a moment, Jericho's intense gaze didn't move away from Edward. It was almost as if Jericho didn't want to give up looking at Edward and, damn, that was the sort of thing that really messed with Edward's head. Jericho finally met Sandy's stare. "It's nice to meet you, Sandy. I'm Jericho."

Sandy smiled like an idiot. "Damn. Wow. Hi, Jericho." She shook his hand. "We usually don't have this much PDA at the local library, especially with the employees, but I'll make an exception this one time."

Jericho smiled.

Edward's knees weakened.

AVERAGE

"Sorry. I forgot where we were."

For a moment, Edward wondered if he would melt into a puddle and if anyone would blame him if he did.

Sandy seemed every bit as wowed by Jericho. "It happens. You should get out of here before it happens again."

With a smile, Jericho grabbed Edward's hand and headed for the door. Edward glanced behind him in time to see Sandy give him two thumbs up and a bright smile. He knew his face had to be every bit as red as it felt.

Jericho didn't stop moving.

Fog overcame them as they stepped outside, freeing Edward from his embarrassment. "Wow. I can't believe this weather. This is nuts."

Jericho led Edward to a black BMW X7. "Why don't I drive you home and then I can bring you to work in the morning?" He held Edward's stare, looking like a devil about to lead Edward to his doom. Jericho brought Edward's hand to his lips while he held his gaze. "It would make me feel better knowing you're not driving in this."

As if Edward would let him out of his sight. "Sounds good." Even as Edward agreed and all sorts of possessiveness rose inside him, gay panic set in. He would probably have to take off his clothes in front of this beautiful man, and Edward didn't think he was that brave. Damn. The doors unlocked and Jericho opened the door for him. Edward scrambled inside before he did anything dumb... like run for his life.

While Jericho circled the vehicle, Edward eyed the inside of the SUV. It was ridiculously nice. He hadn't known biohazard specialists made so much money. Then again, he got the feeling Jericho was a little higher in the company than he let on. It was like humble was all Jericho knew how to be. Edward would toot his horn if he couldn't.

"This is a really nice car," Edward said the moment Jericho slid behind the wheel.

"Um. Yeah. Thanks." Jericho was across the console in an instant, covering Edward's mouth again. Their tongues clashed. Edward kept pulling him closer, trying to touch him everywhere. Jericho smelled amazing. Edward expected he would wake from this dream any minute. Then Jericho's mouth moved to

Edward's neck and Edward heard himself gasp. Everything took on a surreal edge.

"Tell me why I can't stop thinking about you."

Edward wished he knew how to answer that question. He knew why he couldn't stop thinking about Jericho, but he couldn't even begin to guess why anyone would think of him.

"Half of me wants to take you home and fuck you for the rest of the night. The other half wants to take you out to dinner and show you off, so the world knows you're mine. Tell me which to do because I don't know what's right when I'm touching you."

Edward didn't hesitate. "Take me home tonight and I'll take you to dinner tomorrow night."

Jericho leaned away and met his stare, as if checking to ensure he heard correctly. Edward didn't look away.

With a nod, Jericho started the car. "All I need is an address."

It was that easy. Edward knew his mind. If they went to dinner and Jericho never called again, Edward would regret for the rest of his life not making love to Jericho while he had the chance. But if he made love to Jericho and never heard from him again, Edward would be hurt but have no regrets. There was no comparison in his mind. He wanted this. No going back now. In fact, he couldn't wait to break his own heart.

When Jericho pictured dating Edward, he imagined himself slowly luring Edward from his shell. He pictured quitting his job with Zander so he never had to confess to a bigger life of crime than sex work. Jericho imagined a normal nine-to-five life where maybe they got a dog someday. Now Jericho moved at breakneck speed because—more likely than not—he was about to be the next Don of the east coast. He hadn't told Zander yes, but he didn't think he could say no. Edward had better love him before then, or Jericho stood zero chance of keeping him once he was a fucking crime lord.

AVERAGE

As confident as Edward had sounded when he chose a night with Jericho, he practically danced in place as he led Jericho through the door of his apartment. Jericho eyed his every move. He didn't miss the way Edward twisted his fingers or the way he kept biting his lip. Edward was a runner. He might change his mind at any moment. Jericho couldn't let that happen. He had days, not weeks, before Zander would want an answer. Jericho had his heart set on Edward. He had been watching Edward for months, plotting his move. Now life looked short. Jericho stalked Edward through the door like a panther ready to pounce.

"Can I get you some—"

Jericho snatched Edward off his feet, tossed him over his shoulder, and kicked the front door closed. "Which way to the bedroom?"

"Down the hall to the left."

Jericho didn't waste time. Life felt too short. Much shorter than he liked at the moment. Desperation filled his soul. He spotted the black comforter with red flowers. Jericho sat Edward on the edge of the bed.

Edward stared up at him, looking scared as hell. "Are you a Scorpio too?"

"Yes." Jericho snagged Edward's jacket and peeled it off. He had always wondered if he got overheated, dressing in three-piece suits at the library.

"When is your birthday?"

"October twenty-ninth."

Edward blinked. "Wow. Mine's the twenty-seventh. That's wild."

"Yes. Wild." Jericho's fingers went for the top button of Edward's shirt.

Edward stopped him. "I don't look like you."

That was enough. Jericho straddled Edward's body, toppling him backward as he ripped open the two halves of Edward's shirt on the way down. Buttons went flying in every direction as Jericho's mouth covered Edward's. He'd had enough of Edward's insecurities. No more talking. It was time for Edward to see how much Jericho wanted him. Some reactions a person couldn't fake. Holy shit. He had a hairy chest. Jericho hadn't been expecting that.

"Goddamn." He licked a path down Edward's chest and sucked his nipples. Jericho worked on Edward's belt and pants while he nibbled his way downward.

Edward buried his fingers in Jericho's hair. "I've begged God for you."

It was like getting punched in the chest. Jericho's gaze shot to Edward's. Edward looked completely horrified by his own confession. Jericho took a breath. There was no way Edward could understand. Jericho's throat swelled and burned. No one cared about him. No one wanted to keep him. He was a chess piece on a board, maybe, but he wasn't the heart beating in anyone's chest. Jericho crawled back up Edward's body and reclaimed his mouth. This time, he moved slower. Edward deserved to have someone make love to him.

Edward tugged at Jericho's shirt. Jericho let him have it. His pants loosened.

While they kissed, their clothes disappeared as they worked to get closer to each other. A shaky-sounding breath escaped Jericho when their bare skin met. Their fingers linked. He couldn't get enough of exploring Edward's mouth. Jericho forced himself to move away long enough to find a condom and dig through the drawer of Edward's nightstand for lube. Edward somehow looked turned on and embarrassed at the same time. His lips were swollen from Jericho's kisses, but he wouldn't meet Jericho's stare. Yet his gaze kept moving toward where Jericho rolled on the condom. It was obvious he wanted to be braver.

Jericho took Edward's hand and led it to his cock. "It's okay. I want you to touch me. Feel how hard I am for you. I can't fake that."

Edward lightly brushed his fingers down Jericho's erection, as if too nervous to do more.

Jericho handed him the lube. "Touch me."

He squirted some on his fingers and licked his lips. Edward's gaze stayed locked on his task as he swiped the lube down Jericho's length, tentatively at first. With the first pass out of the way, Edward's fingers encircled Jericho's dick.

Jericho moaned.

Edward's gaze lifted. They held each other's stare as Edward coated Jericho's cock with lube. "It's literally been years since there's been anything but toys inside me."

Jericho understood how much that confession cost Edward. "I won't hurt you."

Edward nodded. "I know."

Jericho had never seen so much trust in anyone's eyes. It was humbling. He moved slowly, covering Edward's body with his. Their gazes never wavered. Jericho drew Edward's knees up and toyed with his asshole. He swiped his lubed cock up and down Edward's crack, easing his path. Edward's every breath came out sounding labored. Jericho wanted moans. He stretched Edward's asshole with his fingers, sliding two inside, and mimicking sex. Jericho massaged the spot he knew would make Edward writhe. A tiny mewling sound came from the back of Edward's throat. Jericho hid a triumphant smile. He pulled out his fingers and grabbed his cock. A needy cry escaped Edward. He visibly tried to bite it back. Jericho watched Edward's every reaction as he positioned his crown against Edward's asshole and pushed. Edward's greedy asshole sucked him inside.

A moan tore from Jericho as he slid root-deep inside Edward. For a moment, he closed his eyes and savored his position. He had sat near Edward at the tea shop for months, trying to catch his attention. Now he was inside the man. It felt a lot like winning. Jericho took a breath, pulled almost all the way out, and slammed inside again. A loud moan caressed his ear, driving him to do it again. In no time, he couldn't stop. Sweat coated his skin as he rode Edward's ass. The sound of skin slapping filled the room, mixing with their moans.

AVERAGE

"You're so beautiful. Please don't stop."

Jericho didn't need to be asked. "That's not happening. I need you to come for me. I want your cum dripping from my skin."

"God, you feel so good."

Jericho kissed Edward because he couldn't stop. He felt carnal, and—honestly—he had robbed Edward of quite a bit of foreplay tonight. Jericho had needed to be inside of him too badly. He needed to keep Edward distracted with kisses. Jericho's mind was quickly turning against him—the way it always did. This was why he hadn't had sex in years.

Jericho turned his head away and buried his face in the crook of Edward's neck. "I'm so sorry. You deserved a better night than this. I should've made you dinner with candles and music." Tears pressed at the backs of Jericho's eyes. He was no better than the men who used him. "How are you supposed to understand I care if I do shit like this?"

"Shhh."

Edward's mouth found his.

Jericho sniffed.

Everything slowed and Jericho found himself on his back with Edward straddling his body. Jericho massaged Edward's cock while Edward rocked himself on Jericho's erection. Their lips kept meeting and clinging. A tear rolled back in Jericho's hair. He sniffed again, trying to hold himself together. Then a stuttered-sounding breath fell from Edward's lips and Jericho's mood shifted again. He needed Edward to blow. Jericho stroked faster. Edward braced himself on Jericho's chest and used his body.

With his head thrown back, Edward sucked air and took what he wanted. Jericho couldn't look away. He pumped Edward's cock like he jacked off his own dick. Jericho pumped faster and faster. He swore the closer Edward got, the closer he got to the edge—like Edward's orgasm was his. Then a cry rent the air and Edward's asshole sucked him deep. An orgasm ripped from him, causing the air to seize in his lungs. Jericho couldn't make a sound or move. He held Edward's hips in a death grip as his cock twitched inside Edward's ass. Edward stared at him as he came. They were connected, and Jericho felt whole. Then Edward kissed him, and Jericho's heart melted. He really belonged to this man. Edward just hadn't realized it yet. When he did, Jericho hoped he took it easy on him. Jericho's life had already been a hard one. He just really wanted this soft place to land. Jericho needed Edward.

There had come a moment when Jericho had been kissing a path down Edward's chest that reality had set in. Edward had stopped hoping this was real and begun dreaming it could be forever. That had been the most powerful and terrifying moment of his life. Then—before he had known it would happen—that confession had popped out about begging God for this. He had. So many nights, Edward had lain awake and literally pled with any deity listening to take the loneliness away. To not make him spend the rest of his life with this emptiness. Then Jericho had appeared from nowhere, and Edward couldn't deny the truth. Jericho was the miracle he had been waiting for. He was so much better than anything Edward could have dreamed for himself.

Edward couldn't stop watching Jericho in his sleep. He was such a beautiful mixture of harsh lines and sweet softness. There was a kindness to his face while his torso belonged to a man who had seen terrible things. Edward wanted to hold him and keep him safe. Without thinking, Edward's hand lifted. His fingers traced the horns of the demonic-looking tattoo on his chest. Part of Edward wanted to hear every story of Jericho's past. Mostly, Edward was afraid of what he would hear. Nothing he learned could scare him away, but it might break his heart. He had a bad feeling Jericho had been tortured in ways Edward couldn't even imagine. Edward couldn't bear that.

Jericho's gorgeous eyes opened and focused on him.

Guilt washed over Edward for waking him. "Sorry."

A smirk touched Jericho's lips. He rolled and tucked Edward beneath him before smothering him in kisses. Edward laughed and fought for his life, but not really, since he lived for every second. Finally, Jericho fell still. His kisses turned sweet on Edward's neck.

"I didn't mean to fall asleep. Jet lag got the best of me."

"You don't have to explain." Edward stroked Jericho's hair. "Go back to sleep. I'm enjoying this part more than you know."

Jericho's hand ran down Edward's body, as if he savored every inch. "No. I need to get up and find you some dinner. You can't go to bed without eating. I don't want to throw off your nightly routine. That's not healthy."

Edward laughed. He couldn't stop himself. For the first time in his life, he was just too happy to contain it. He patted his stomach. "I can afford to miss a meal. You can't afford to lose any sleep."

"No." Jericho pretended to cry as he moved down Edward's body and cradled his stomach. "I must protect this beautiful form. It's so sexy." He kissed Edward's stomach, as if worshipping it.

Edward shook with laughter. Then Jericho's kisses turned hotter, and Edward realized he was serious. Jericho was genuinely aroused by Edward's body. He watched in fascination as Jericho caressed his chest hair and kissed his way back to Edward's mouth. His expression screamed desire. For the first time in Edward's life, he felt true power run through his veins. All because of this beautiful man. Edward had thought he could handle a single night with the possibility of never hearing from Jericho again. He couldn't. Edward would stalk this man to the ends of the earth now. As their tongues met and stroked, Edward already planned their entire future. It looked beautiful. Now all Edward had to do was make it come true. He would.

Chapter Five

THE CONTENTS OF EDWARD'S refrigerator were his only guide. While Edward showered and got ready for work, Jericho cooked breakfast and packed Edward a lunch. He found brown paper bags in the cabinet and sandwich bags in the drawer by the stove. There was fresh bread in the breadbox and lunch meat in the fridge. He found carrot sticks, applesauce and cookies. Plus, some chips and a yogurt. There was a plastic cutlery package from a takeout place in his silverware drawer, so Jericho tossed that in the bag too.

"Oh my gosh. Did you make biscuits from scratch? I didn't even know I had the stuff to do that."

Jericho turned to find Edward ready for work. He wore his usual jacket and button-down shirt. His brown hair had a hint of curl. He was adorable. "Oh dear. Will I get you in trouble at work?"

Edward blinked. "Why? Do I have a hickey or something?"

Jericho crossed the room and hauled Edward into his arms. "No, because I'm about to make you late."

Laughter flashed in Edward's eyes as Jericho claimed his lips. His hands found Edward's ass and squeezed. He had only been teasing about making

AVERAGE

Edward late, but now he didn't know if he could stop touching him. Edward's stomach growled, giving him the strength he needed to pull away.

"Mhmm. I guess I should let you eat. I can be patient."

Edward clung to Jericho's shirt. "Maybe I can't."

Damn. "Eat. I'll take you to work, and then when I pick you up tonight, you can have your way with me."

"Nope." Edward pulled away and moved to the table. "I said I would take you to dinner tonight and I am. No arguing."

Jericho set a plate of food in front of him and hid a smile. "Yes, sir, but I'll still pick you up."

"Fair enough."

With a shake of his head, Jericho moved to clean up his mess. He had a lot to do today if he hoped to be back to get Edward on time. By the time he finished cleaning the kitchen, Edward had cleaned his plate and was ready to go.

Jericho handed him his lunch.

Edward blinked. "You packed me a lunch?"

"Of course."

With a blank expression, Edward clutched the bag to his chest and headed to Jericho's SUV in silence. He looked like Jericho had left him speechless.

Jericho couldn't stop shaking his head. He didn't understand Edward. He acted like no one had ever done anything nice for him. Halfway to the library, Jericho couldn't take the silence any longer. "Are you okay?"

With the lunch sack still clutched to his chest, Edward glanced his way. "Yes. Of course. Why?"

"You haven't said a word since we left."

Edward cleared his throat. It was an uncomfortable sound. "I'm just in shock, I suppose. In a good way," he thankfully tacked on before Jericho ended up too confused. "I've been alone for a long time. Meeting you has been a bit of a whirlwind. My brain is still trying to process how good you are to me."

Jericho was back to being confused. "You act like no one else is ever nice to you."

"They're not." Edward said the words too fast for them to be a lie. He immediately tried to backtrack. "I mean, my boss is good to me, and we hang out sometimes outside of work. But at the end of the day, she's still my boss and I think that would win out if anything went wrong."

"What about your parents?"

A loud snort rent the air. Edward covered his mouth. "Sorry. I almost hurt myself with that one. Um. Let's see…" Edward fell silent.

Jericho chanced a quick glance his way.

Edward stared into space as if trying to recall something before finally speaking again. "I think it was like three days after I graduated from college, my mom called to tell me I had to do this church thing she had arranged. Because I'm an adult, I said no. She said she was my mom, and I didn't get to say no. I reminded her I was an adult, and I would do what I damned well pleased. She fell into a lecture on my godly duties to my elders and I told her I was gay just to shut her up. The silence was pretty freaking deafening. Then, she hung up on me and I never heard from her again."

Jericho fought the urge to rub his chest where an ache began. Despite Edward's cavalier tone, Jericho swore he felt the knife go through Edward's heart. "How long ago was that?"

"Seven years. Honestly, it was for the best, though. She was super abusive. Everyone knew it and no one ever did anything to stop it. So, no. No one has ever been nice to me."

"Damn." Jericho didn't know what else to say. She didn't deserve him. He pulled into the library parking lot and put the vehicle in park so he could turn Edward's way. "I'm sorry that happened to you. You didn't deserve it."

Edward shrugged, looking uncomfortable. "I knew what would happen if I ever said the words." His gaze moved over Jericho's face. "I had to speak my truth, though, or there was no hope I'd find you."

He had given up a family—shitty or not—on pure faith of finding another. Jericho wouldn't let him regret that decision. "I have you now. Get used to being spoiled."

A sweet smile touched Edward's lips. He visibly tried to squelch it. "Have a good day. I'll see you after work."

Jericho nodded. "Kiss me first."

AVERAGE

Edward leaned across the console and whisked his lips across Jericho's. Jericho captured Edward's mouth before he got away. Their tongues brushed. His heart soared. As much as Jericho didn't want to stop and let Edward go, he knew he had to let him get to work. He pulled away and pressed his forehead against Edward's. "Have a good day, gorgeous. Text me if you get bored."

While fighting a blush, Edward slipped from the vehicle and headed for the door. Jericho watched him move toward where Sandy waited. Halfway there, Edward held up his lunch sack and Sandy covered her mouth. Jericho chuckled at the sight. He didn't look away until Edward was safely in the building. His happiness didn't dampen until he was completely alone with his thoughts.

Jericho tapped the screen on his dashboard, pulling up his contacts, until he found Zander's name. He hit the call icon. Ringing filled the speakers.

"Hello?"

"I'll take the job."

A moment of silence met Jericho's announcement. Finally, Zander sighed. Jericho didn't know if it was in relief or exhaustion. "Put together your team."

"Already on it."

Another beat of silence met his claim. Zander took an audible breath. "I know this isn't easy for you."

"The money will make it easier."

A soft chuckle rang through the speakers. "That's true. How's the librarian?"

AVERAGE

Jericho's gaze moved toward the door of the library. He took a breath as images of their night together filled his mind. "He's perfect."

"Good. Having the right man at your side will mean everything."

"I know," Jericho said without hesitation. "That's the only reason I said yes."

"Keep me posted on your next move."

"I will." Jericho disconnected the call and dialed Dante next.

Dante didn't say hello. "What's up?"

Jericho got it. He never called. No doubt, Dante expected something was wrong. "Are you home? We need to talk."

"Yeah. Come on by."

"I'll be there soon." Jericho put the car in reverse and disconnected the call at the same time. The library wasn't far from Dante and Marshall's place. It didn't take him long to get there. Still, Dante had coffee waiting as he let Jericho inside.

Dante gathered his long blond hair and pulled it up before dropping it again, in a show of nerves, as he sat across from Jericho at the kitchen table. "What's going on? You never call or stop by."

Jericho didn't leave him hanging. He knew they all had bad anxiety, but he hadn't wanted to stop by unannounced. "The team is being disbanded."

Dante ran his tongue across his teeth, obviously barely clinging to his temper. "So Zander decided to fire me after all. He didn't even have the balls to do it himself the way he did Wulf. I don't know what the fuck he expected. Wulf and Beau are my brothers—"

"You're not fired," Jericho said, cutting Dante off before he got too riled.

"Oh."

Jericho took a breath. "Zander has asked me to take over the east coast, as him."

Dante's eyes widened. "What?" He dragged out the question, sounding like Jericho had felt since the moment Zander called him to California.

"I've accepted."

Somehow, Dante's eyes got bigger.

Jericho kept going because he had to start somewhere. "This means you have a choice to make. One, you can have my old job as the lead coordinator. Ender will call you with the details of upcoming operations, and you schedule the teams to go in for cleanup. Or, two, you can accept the full-time position as my right-hand man."

Dante sat back, blinking. "Whoa."

A small smile touched Jericho's lips. "Wulf and you are my brothers. You two have been my team for years. Obviously, I'd love for Wulf to be at my side too, but he wants a normal life now, so I want that for him too. It's just us left now. If you want to stick with what you know, I understand. I don't know what I've gotten myself into, but Zander told me to build my new team. There's nowhere else I'd rather start. There's no one I trust more."

Dante nodded. It wasn't an answer. Jericho knew Dante would need time to think. Likely, he would need to talk things over with Marshall, but Jericho felt better just being here.

AVERAGE

"You're the right man for the job."

The confidence in Dante's voice had Jericho's shoulders relaxing. Dante had no idea how much Jericho needed to hear those words. Nothing felt right beyond Edward at the moment. He needed Dante at his side. He needed someone who believed in him. God knew, he didn't believe in himself. In Jericho's mind, he would always be the strung-out prostitute one bad day away from the streets. The more people keeping him sane the better. For everyone.

It had been a long day, waiting to get back to Jericho. No one could possibly understand. Jericho had packed him lunch. When Edward was a kid, he had watched other kids eat while he went hungry at school until he learned to forge his mother's signature and fill out the paperwork for a free lunch. If school had been out for any reason, he had gone without again. It wasn't because his mom couldn't afford to buy food. She thought Edward had too much potential to be fat, and she had to nip it in the bud.

A single night with Jericho had really made Edward a mess. He couldn't stop thinking about the way Jericho had worshipped all the things about him that Edward had always hated. Now Edward didn't know what was real anymore. He had spent the past seven years trying to cut his mom's voice from his head, but he wasn't sure which was hers and what had become his at this point. She had taught him to hate himself. It was a lesson he didn't know if he could unlearn.

As Edward headed toward the door at five, there was more than a little trepidation in his heart. If Jericho wasn't waiting for him, then it meant those voices in his head were right, and he had been an easy mark because of it. The final steps almost snapped his sanity. Then he pushed open the door and his knees nearly buckled. Outside the library sat a fountain. People used it as a wishing well. Every few years, the library voted on a charity to donate the change to when it overwhelmed the sculpted piece. In a suit that likely cost as much as the SUV Jericho drove, Jericho stood near the fountain eyeing it, as if confused by its existence. Edward's knees felt like noodles as he moved Jericho's way. He was too fucking gorgeous to be real. If Sandy hadn't spent the day gushing over every detail of him with Edward, Edward would swear he dreamed Jericho.

"Hi."

At his greeting, Jericho's light blue gaze turned his way. He lit from the inside and Edward melted. Surely, he had been a great man in another lifetime to have been given this miracle because Edward had not earned Jericho in this life.

"Hey." Jericho pointed at the fountain. "Has this always been here? I swear I didn't see it last night."

Edward's face hurt from smiling. He hadn't stopped all day. "It was foggy last night."

Jericho's confused expression didn't clear. "Why is there change in it?"

The question confused Edward. "It's a wishing well."

"But it isn't a well."

That was a valid point. "Yeah, I don't know. At some point, people just started tossing coins in fountains instead of wells and making wishes. I don't know the lore behind it. It's just a thing people do. Have you never heard of wishing wells?"

Jericho shrugged. "This sounds like a kid's thing. I was never a kid."

A pain punched Edward in the chest, knocking the wind from his lungs. There were likely millions of tiny things Jericho had never experienced that were completely normal and taken for granted by everyone else. Edward couldn't fathom the life he had lived. He wished he could give him back some of what he lost.

Edward dug a coin from his pocket and held it out to Jericho. "Take this, make a wish, and then toss it in the fountain. The deity guarding this fountain will grant your wish."

A childlike smile touched Jericho's lips as he accepted the coin. He took a step closer to Edward. "I wish I could keep you forever." Jericho's gaze never wavered from Edward's as he made his wish aloud before tossing the coin into the fountain.

Edward didn't have it in his heart to tell Jericho he was supposed to make his wish silently. Honestly, he didn't give a shit about anything but the way Jericho looked at him and the words still ringing in his ears. Surely this man wasn't real. That was the only thought that kept bombarding Edward all hours of the days since Jericho appeared in his life. How had Edward walked this earth so many years without knowing such a man existed outside the books he read? He kept waiting for the other shoe to drop. There had to be something truly terrible around the corner. No way were things this perfect.

"Tell me now—before I find out the hard way—what is it about you that's going to break me? There's no way you're this amazing. Good things don't happen to me."

"I'll never let anything bad happen to you."

Edward's hands found Jericho's chest because he had to touch him. "You look so sexy in this suit. What have you been doing today?"

"I took the promotion."

A smile snapped to Edward's lips. He shuffled closer. "Really? There's no chance you'll go back to California?"

Jericho looked entirely too serious. He stroked Edward's cheek. "None. Are you going to kiss me? I feel like I've been waiting a really long time."

Happiness poured from Edward. He laughed as he lunged forward and claimed Jericho's lips. Then he felt Jericho smile, as if Jericho hadn't truly been happy until Edward held him. Edward didn't know if his heart would hold out. He had never been this happy. His body might not have what it took to contain it. He would damn well try, though.

"Let's go celebrate. Tell me where I'm taking you to dinner so I can publicly laud your amazing accomplishments."

Jericho took his hand and headed toward his SUV. "I have an idea, but we should change first."

"Okay. Why? What should I wear?"

Jericho flashed him a childish grin. "You've got me in a mood now with all this wishing business. Let's go to Carnival Park."

An unexpected hint of excitement shot through Edward. "Okay." He scrambled into Jericho's vehicle. He never did anything fun. Edward had no one to go anywhere with and he couldn't recall the last time he had been to Carnival Park. It really wasn't much more than a tourist district with carnival style rides and food trucks, but they also had several shops. He wasn't big on the rides, but he loved the food trucks and garish tourist shops. Edward enjoyed walking the strip and looking at the novelty items. It wasn't fun alone, but that sounded like the perfect way to celebrate Jericho's promotion.

"How do you want to do this? Changing clothes, I mean," Edward clarified. "Your place is closer to Carnival Park, but I don't have any clothes there."

Jericho backed from his parking space. "We'll go to your place first. You can pack a bag." He looked Edward's way as he shifted into drive. "For as many nights as you'd like to stay." Jericho emphasized each word, as if ensuring Edward understood he had meant his wish. When he went back to watching the road, Edward pressed his hand to his stomach to calm the butterflies. Jericho continued. "Then we'll go to my place to change before heading out for the night. Does that work for you?"

"Yeah. I'm good with that." More than good. He was ecstatic. Edward rode his euphoria all the way to his apartment. Jericho waited in the car while Edward ran inside and packed a bag. Because he was filled with all the wishful thinking, he grabbed three days' worth of clothes and watered his plants. His car was still parked at the library. Edward wasn't sure he cared if he ever saw it again. A crazy desire built inside him to never look back. He wanted to beg Jericho to keep driving and let him take this new happiness and build a better life from scratch. As much as he loved his job, he craved something more sometimes. He swore meeting Jericho had finally made him believe he could be someone different.

Those thoughts carried him inside Jericho's house, distracting him until Jericho peeled off his jacket. That was all it took to bring Edward back to a reality he loved. Jericho had wished to keep him forever. Damn. He was afraid of the hunger in his heart at that moment.

Jericho turned and froze.

They held each other's stare.

Edward didn't know what Jericho saw in his eyes, but he could guess. He had never been good at hiding his emotions. They still stood inside the kitchen, having barely cleared the back door. He had just taken off his shoes. The door still stood open half an inch at his back. Then Edward's body collided with the door, slamming it shut when Jericho overcame him. Jericho's tall frame seemed to be everywhere at once. He tore at Edward's clothes. His mouth explored Edward's, tongues stroking. There was zero blood left in Edward's brain. It had all rushed to his dick the moment Jericho's body molded against him.

"We're going out. I swear," Jericho vowed as he dropped to his knees.

Edward didn't have time to reassure Jericho, he believed, before Jericho swallowed his cock. The whole thing. All the way to the root. Edward didn't know how he stayed upright. A sound escaped he had never made before. Jericho's gaze flipped upward. His hair stood in every direction. He held Edward's stare as he sucked Edward's dick. It was the hottest moment of Edward's life, and he lost part of himself to Jericho right then. He felt it happen. They weren't a fling. This wasn't a fluke. Jericho wasn't toying with him. This was real. There was no going back.

Chapter Six

JERICHO: *HOW IS WORK going?*

Edward: *Okay. We got a ton of donations over the weekend. I've been sorting them all day. I feel gross.*

Jericho: *After I pick you, I'll give you a bath before feeding you tonight.*

Edward: *I'm too spoiled already.*

Jericho: *Not yet.*

Edward: *Sandy asked if my car has moved in the six weeks since we've started dating. I don't know why, but I lied and said yes. Lol.*

Jericho: *Do you want me to have someone take it to your apartment?*

Edward: *Nah. You never know. I might want to go out for lunch one day.*

Jericho: *If so, call me. I might want to go too.*

Edward: *Okay. Want to go to lunch today?*

Jericho: *Yes. How did you know?*

Edward: *LOL! Lucky guess.*

AVERAGE

Jericho: *These people keep asking questions about subway tile and barn doors. Are these real things in people's homes? I feel very out of my league while designing this new house Zander says I need.*

Edward: *While I still don't understand why a new job requires a new house, other than you can afford it, you drive a hundred-thousand-dollar vehicle. Why don't you know about subway tile and barn doors?*

Jericho: *Do you?*

Edward: *Yes. But I've been dreaming about designing my own place since I moved into my first apartment so it's probably not fair to ask me.*

Jericho: *It's your lucky day then. Tell Sandy you have an emergency. You have to help me design your new home.*

Edward: *What?*

Jericho: *Surely you didn't think I planned to live in this massive place alone, did you?*

Edward: *Did you just ask me to move in with you over a text message?*

Jericho: *I'm standing outside by the fountain. Come outside and I'll ask you to your face.*

Come outside and I'll ask you to your face. Those words carried Edward's feet to the front door of the library without him thinking to ask for permission to leave. Edward was too fucked up. He had been dating Jericho for four months, but they hadn't exchanged any words of love or talked about moving in together. They spent every night together. In fact, they spent every waking moment together that they weren't working, but still, Edward hadn't seen this coming. Sure enough, Jericho stood outside by the fountain, looking vulnerable—like he genuinely didn't know shit about subway tile, and he expected Edward would reject him. As if Edward knew how.

Edward still held his phone as he moved to stand toe to toe with Jericho.

With his hands in the pockets of his jeans, Jericho held his stare. His light blue t-shirt made his light blue eyes pop.

Edward might have sighed if he wasn't still in shock. "Did you really ask me to move in with you?"

"Yes."

"Why?" Even Edward heard the confusion in his voice.

A line appeared between Jericho's eyebrows. "What do you mean, why? We have already practically lived together now for the past four months. I love you. I don't want to build this new life alone."

Edward's fingers went numb. His phone hit the pavement.

Jericho retrieved it, while all Edward could do was stare at nothing in shock. "Damn. The screen shattered. I guess this is a good time to add you to my phone plan."

Edward blinked. "What is happening?"

For a moment, Jericho stared at him in silence. He shook his head, as if Edward made him tired. "Do you love me?"

Edward didn't hesitate. "Of course."

"Do you want to move in with me?"

"Yes." Edward didn't have any trouble answering when asked directly. His brain just didn't want to work properly.

"Then go tell Sandy you need the rest of the day off and we'll get you a new phone."

"Okay."

Edward turned to go, but Jericho stopped him. "Hold on. Kiss me first."

Their lips brushed and reality sank in finally. Edward took a shuddered breath. "I love you."

Jericho's lips shaped a smile against his as he came in for another quick kiss. "I love you too." Jericho sent Edward on his way back inside with a little pat on the ass.

Edward walked inside in a daze. His gaze immediately found Sandy's behind the counter.

She rolled her eyes. "I've already clocked you out for the day."

He didn't look a gift horse in the mouth. Edward ran for his life. He knew Sandy had started getting irritated with him a few weeks ago, and it grew a little more every day. She wasn't wrong. Jericho had eclipsed everything since they started dating. He had gone from never missing a single day of work or taking extended lunch breaks to being the shittiest worker she had. Edward kept telling himself he would do better tomorrow. Then, like now, he took one look at Jericho, and ruining his life meant nothing. In fact, as he walked back outside and into Jericho's arms, he didn't think he cared if Sandy fired him tomorrow.

Jericho kissed his ear.

Edward's eyes fell closed at the sensation. He wanted to stay like this forever.

"Now tell me why everyone wants to know if I want barn doors in the new house."

"You don't," Edward said against Jericho's shoulder. "They start rolling open on their own accord while you're sitting on the toilet and you're helpless to do anything to stop it."

Jericho's body shook with laughter, making Edward smile. "Why does this sound personal?"

"It is. My grandmother used to have them on all her bathrooms."

With his arm draped over Edward's shoulders, Jericho steered him toward the parking lot. "Good to know. Normal doors on all the rooms. See. It's a good thing I have you to save me."

"Maybe not all the rooms. I've always thought a swinging pantry door would be cute."

Jericho nodded, looking thoughtful. "I like it. We'll work on it together."

The driver's side door opened on a black Land Rover. A man in a dark suit and sunglasses opened the back door for Edward. "Hey, Edward. How was work?"

It took Edward a moment to realize it was Dante. Dante was Jericho's assistant and spent a lot of time with Jericho, but this was new.

"Um. Good. How's your day going?"

"Great."

Edward cast Jericho a questioning glance.

Jericho motioned him inside the waiting SUV. After Edward climbed inside, Dante closed the door. Dante opened the door for Jericho, and he climbed in next to Edward. Jericho acted as if this was how he was treated all day while Edward worked. Edward couldn't stop blinking like an owl and watching the pomp and circumstance.

The moment the door closed, but before Dante made it back to the driver's seat, Edward's curiosity exploded. "What the fuck just happened? Since when is Dante opening doors and driving us places?"

Jericho brought Edward's hand to his lips, distracting him. "You knew things would change," he answered quietly between kisses. His mouth moved from Edward's knuckles to the inside of his wrist. "Isn't this better? I get to focus on you while Dante drives."

It wasn't like Edward could argue. He didn't know why he cared, honestly. It wasn't his money. Things were just changing so rapidly. This wasn't the same Jericho he had met at the tea shop. Yet, he was. The money hadn't changed Jericho. Not yet. But it became clearer every day that this promotion was a tremendous change in circumstances that most people never saw—like winning the lottery.

"This doesn't feel weird to you?"

Jericho kissed his way toward the bend in Edward's arm, making his smile grow. "Are you distracted yet because I'm tired of thinking about work?"

Edward bit his bottom lip. He couldn't even imagine the stress Jericho was under now. Edward decided right then he would always be Jericho's peace. "What were we talking about?"

A sexy soft chuckle rumbled from Jericho, making goosebumps rise on Edward's skin. "There are samples all over my living room of tile and flooring. What do you think about getting coffee and snacks before we dive into decorating our dream home?"

"Okay."

Jericho didn't look away from Edward. "Then I'll buy you dinner when we're done."

"Okay."

"Then you can sit on my lap and read to me."

Edward couldn't stop smiling. "Okay."

"Until I distract you."

"As always," Edward said with a laugh. He had no complaints. Edward loved their life together. He could get used to them having a driver while Jericho focused on him. Edward could get used to anything, as long as he had Jericho.

Jericho hadn't known how to spring the major shift in his life on Edward other than to literally spring it on him. He had spent the day completely overwhelming Edward, making him choose flooring, windows, and backsplash. Edward had looked at floor plans, worked on custom bathroom fixtures and closet space for their bedroom. Jericho had given him carte blanche over everything, including a library space. Edward was already half asleep by the time they were showered, and he relaxed in Jericho's lap with their latest book.

Jericho made it through five pages. "What would you say if I asked you to quit your job?" The question had been on the tip of his tongue for weeks. Soon, Edward wouldn't be safe to continue working outside Jericho's home. Once word spread of Jericho's new role and the wrong people learned Edward existed, his life wouldn't be the same.

Silence met his question.

Jericho held his breath and waited. He wouldn't push, but he needed this answer.

After a moment, Edward cleared his throat. "I'm not sure what you're asking me exactly."

Honestly, Jericho wasn't sure either. He only knew Edward couldn't stay at the library. "I'm asking you to let me take care of you."

"In what way?"

AVERAGE

Even though Edward was sprawled across his lap in the recliner, Edward didn't look directly at him as he made the inquiry. Jericho didn't know what Edward hid from him. That part mattered.

He tucked two fingers beneath Edward's chin and lifted, forcing Edward to meet his stare. His breath caught at the hope and fear he saw in Edward's eyes. The truth washed over Jericho. Edward wanted to say yes, but he was scared shitless Jericho would steal everything from him, then leave him high and dry down the road after wrecking him.

"Marry me." Jericho said the words without thinking. They just popped out before he had time to process. He couldn't let Edward fear a future with him. Jericho wasn't going anywhere. He scrambled to make his idea seem less crazy. "It doesn't have to be right now. We can have a long engagement, if you want. I just want you to know this is forever. You can quit and I'll take care of you. I want this." Jericho motioned between them, trying to explain he wanted to do this every night for the rest of his life. "I want it forever."

"Okay. I mean, yes. I want that too."

"Yes, you'll quit? Or yes, you'll marry me?"

Edward shrugged. "Both."

A smile exploded across Jericho's face. He tried to temper his reaction even though happiness completely owned him. "I know I'm asking everything of you. I promise you, I will always be worth it."

A blinding smile lit Edward's face. "That I don't doubt for a second." He bit his bottom lip, looking adorably guilty. "I think Sandy is about to fire me anyhow, honestly."

"Thank you."

The look of confusion that filled Edward's features nearly made Jericho laugh. "Why are you thanking me for being on the verge of getting fired?"

A chuckle sneaked out before Jericho could stop it. "That's not what I meant. Thank you for always making my life better, brighter, and easier. You have no idea how much it means to me to know you're here."

Edward's open confusion didn't clear. "Of course."

"I'm serious," Jericho said, sounding every bit as resolute as he felt. He needed Edward to understand. "My life has never been steady, and it feels—"Jericho took a shaky breath and tried again. "It feels..."

Edward set his book aside and shifted positions on Jericho's lap. He straddled Jericho's body, holding his stare while he scratched his scalp. "I know it must feel like everything is just barreling ahead without you right now, but you're right. I'm here. If you want me to text Sandy right now and tell her I can't come back, I will. You need me more. They have plenty of part-time people who would pounce on my full-time position in a second. I will sit here with you and read all day. Whatever you need me to do, I'm your man. Honestly, I still have no idea what you do at that company, but I'm willing to help. I'm running on faith here because I have never believed in anything or anyone as much as I trust in you. You've got this."

Goddamn. He was a lucky man. "Turn in your notice. Don't burn a bridge for me. Sandy was your friend before I came along. I don't want to be the reason you lose her."

Edward shifted closer. His expression turned wicked. Jericho's cock stirred. He swore he could read Edward's mind. "I'll meet you in the middle. Tomorrow, I'll go in and talk to Sandy. That way, we can work out a short notice together where I haven't burned a bridge or lost a friend. Then I'll be free to drive you nuts full time."

Jericho's hands found their way inside the back of Edward's pajama pants. "I'm free to be driven nuts right now."

Edward's gaze hooded. He slithered down Jericho's body. Jericho watched it happen with his breath held. He loved seeing the confidence grow in Edward every day. Edward kissed a path to the waistband of Jericho's pajama pants. Jericho's cock was already trying to climb out to reach Edward's mouth. A wicked smile touched Edward's lips as he set Jericho's erection free. Jericho's breath caught at his expression. Sometimes, from nowhere, it would strike him anew how lucky he was to have Edward. Then Edward's lips wrapped around Jericho's cock and Jericho didn't have another clear thought. Edward put his whole heart into blowing Jericho.

Jericho writhed and begged beneath his touch.

"Please. Oh god. That feels so good. I'm so in love with you." Jericho had no idea what he said. It didn't matter. The hot mouth pulling on his dick made him insane. Edward sucked harder and faster. Saliva coated his cock and Edward's chin. Jericho couldn't look away. A cry tore from his throat as the pressure quickly blasted into waves of ecstasy. Edward never pulled away from him.

Jericho shoved his hand inside Edward's pants and tugged Edward's erection, massaging and pulling. He needed Edward to get on the same level of heaven as him. Edward clung to him. Small cries escaped between moans and biting Jericho's chest. Edward didn't try to hide his desire, and that shit always punched Jericho in the heart. He wanted this for the rest of his life. Jericho had the one man he craved going wild in his hand. That was a dream come true for him. As Edward came, crying Jericho's name, Jericho felt a sense of peace wash over him. He would clean Edward's skin and slow things down for a few hours before heating them up again. That was how he planned to addict Edward to being with him. Just in case—once Edward learned the whole truth about him—love wasn't enough. He needed Edward to be hooked.

Chapter Seven

AFTER TAKING SOME TIME to think, Edward gave a two-week notice. Not only that, but he also worked his ass off for those two weeks and talked things over with Sandy before he left. Even though she couldn't guarantee he would have the same position if he returned, she would find a place for him if he ever needed another job. Jericho had been right about not burning a bridge, but maybe not for the reason he meant. The moment Jericho hadn't been holding him any longer, Edward had pan-icked at the idea of being unemployed and completely dependent on Jericho for his every need.

Thankfully, that anxiety had passed the moment his things were packed and moved inside their still under con-struction home. The place was finished enough for them to stay there, but it wasn't easy. There was always a crew under foot, and someone always need-ed Edward's input about last-minute changes or approvals. It felt like Jericho worked around the clock. Men came and went. Jericho came and went. Ed-ward might have come and gone if his car wasn't still at the library, which was almost laughable. He had tried once to bring it home before the end of his no-tice, but the battery had been shot. They had been too busy with the house and

AVERAGE

Jericho's new job for Edward to bring it up to Jericho. Plus, Dante always ended up driving him everywhere anyhow. Edward couldn't even say how it happened. One second, he would mention going somewhere, then boom. Dante would be behind the wheel, and Edward would be on the way. He couldn't complain, since it was nice to not be alone. It seemed like casting longing looks Jericho's way was the closest he got to him until bedtime each night.

Edward was determined today. He headed for Jericho's makeshift, wall-less office downstairs to steal him for the day, or—in the very least—for the morning. They needed some time alone. He found Jericho already in a meeting. Edward's shoulders fell as he spotted Jericho seated across from two men he had never seen. Jericho's gaze moved his way. He winked and went back to chatting with the pair. Edward headed for a nearby set of wingback chairs where he could watch, but was out of earshot. He didn't want to eavesdrop, but he needed Jericho to know he still existed... and he was bored.

Dante appeared at his side and filled the chair next to him. "Did you want to go somewhere?"

Edward cast the blond a quick glance. "Hey. Good morning. No. I just wanted to talk to Jericho, but I didn't know he was in a meeting. Who are these guys?" Normally, Edward wouldn't have asked, but one man looked dangerous. He was solid muscle, and his bald head was covered in tattoos. The man at his side was only slightly smaller, but he looked friendlier.

AVERAGE

"Bear and Creed Lewis."

"Brothers?"

Dante chuckled. "No. They're married."

Edward was more relieved than he cared to admit. Both men were sexy and sexual in a way he couldn't explain. Edward still didn't understand why they were there.

"What are they talking to Jericho about?" Edward whispered the question. He couldn't help it. It felt like he broke some unspoken rule by asking anything at all, but he felt lacking just knowing they sat within feet of Jericho.

"Jericho is trying to convince them to come work for him."

The more questions Dante answered, the more Edward had. No one had told him anything before now. "You don't sound like you think it'll happen."

Dante flashed him a smile and shrugged. He leaned Edward's way and lowered his voice, as if really getting into the conversation. "The bald one is Bear. He's a private contractor who's done years of shadow work for like the CIA and the FBI. He'd be perfect for our company. Zander has tried to hire him for years, but Jericho has leverage Zander didn't: location. See, Creed's parents live here in Cage Beach. Creed used to be a police officer for the Cage Beach Police Department. They moved to Washington after they got married, but Creed's parents have been trying to get them to move back and Bear still has to come here all the time for work. So, I mean, it would actually be perfect for the two of them to accept the job with Jericho and come live here with you two."

"With us? Like here under the same roof? I don't understand. What sort of job would have them living with us?"

Dante's eyebrows drew together. "They'd be your security team."

The more Dante talked, the louder Edward's heartbeat sounded in his ears. He realized how little he knew about his own life. Everything had moved so fast since he met Jericho. He thought he understood what Jericho did, but then again, he didn't. Edward tried to get answers from Dante without seeming clueless.

"Why do we need full-time security? We haven't before now." He purposely tried to phrase his question as if he knew what was going on, but still didn't understand.

Dante's eyed him as if suspicions only deepened. "You know what Jericho does, right?"

Edward forced a hint of confidence he didn't feel into his tone and pieced together the things Jericho had said about work. "Yeah. I mean, I get that he's in charge of the east coast and all, but I didn't realize that would mean a live-in security team."

Dante's shoulders relaxed. His expression cleared. He looked visibly relieved that Edward obviously wasn't completely clueless. "Yeah. Unfortunately, it does. Even though Jericho's job title is technically CEO of the Kapra Foundation, which is the charity that funds the rescue, rehabilitation, and re-homing of sex trafficking victims, once word spreads that he's the one who's running the east coast of this operation, you two won't be safe."

With his gaze locked on the meeting taking place across the room, Edward nodded. He tried to process everything he learned from Dante. Mostly, he wanted to cry. He didn't know how to feel. It seemed like all of that was shit Jericho should have said to him. Edward had thought Jericho had taken over the east coast division of a biohazard company. That was a little funny. Leave it to Jericho to refer to sex traffickers as biohazard. They were, but Edward felt like everything was a lie. He didn't know where to go with that.

"I tried to get my car from the library parking lot, but the battery was dead. Do you think we could do something about that?"

"Yeah," Dante said without missing a beat. "I'll have it towed here and we'll figure it out from there."

Edward nodded. "I appreciate it. Will you take me to the tea shop? I think I need a day away from here."

"Sure thing."

With a final longing glance Jericho's way, Edward headed for the door. He needed some time to think, and he couldn't do it here. Jericho had lied to him, or at least, he thought so. Edward didn't know anything anymore. All he knew was his life had changed more than he realized, and he didn't know if he liked the way things were headed or if he wanted this any longer. Edward needed to get away and clear his head. He needed to think. More than anything, he needed to breathe.

Building a house, changing careers, building an entire team, and getting engaged at the same time had taken an unexpected toll on Jericho in the last six months. He didn't know how Zander had worked nonstop like this for years on end. When he had seen Edward come downstairs during his meeting with Creed and Bear, his heart had soared, only for his hopes to dash the second Edward disappeared again. They were passing ships these days. Jericho worked every second his eyes were open, and Edward handled everything

Jericho couldn't. They were a hell of a team. It was destroying them. Jericho felt the divide growing wider each day. He didn't know how to make it stop.

With an hour between meetings, Jericho snagged the custom-made engagement ring from his desk and stood. An hour might not seem like much, but he could work with that. He slipped the ring inside his pocket. He would corner Edward and toss everyone else out. They couldn't go on like this. Jericho needed to ensure Edward knew how important he was to him. None of this meant shit without his angel at his side.

Jericho made it three steps before Dante came skidding into the room, panting. "We've got a problem."

Jericho's heart rate shot through the roof. His mind immediately went to the worst-case scenario. "Is it Edward? Where is he?"

Dante made a dismissive gesture while trying to catch his breath. "No. I just brought him home from the tea shop. He's upstairs taking a nap, but it's about him. This morning, he asked me if I would retrieve his car from the library. Apparently, he tried to pick it up some time back, but the battery was dead. I called a company to tow it here so we could deal with it."

"Okay." Jericho wasn't following.

"It exploded the moment they moved it. Took half the library out with it."

Jericho's knees weakened. He stared at Dante, feeling nothing and everything at once. Rage won. Someone had tried taking Edward from him. Jericho literally had nothing else he cared about in this world. They had chosen the right target, but they had fucked up by failing. Jericho knew nothing but hatred and fury.

"Find out who did it and bring them here. I don't care what it takes."

Dante nodded. "Already on it. Thankfully, Bear is still in town, and he's got Ransom working overtime too. We won't let anything happen to your man, Jericho. You know this. You're my brother. I'll protect him with my life. Just like I know you would for me."

Jericho nodded, feeling numb. "Thank you. I know and I appreciate you more than you'll ever know. You've been great with Edward."

"He's an amazing guy. You're very lucky. He's going to take this in stride."

Jericho kept nodding because he didn't know what else to do. "Was anyone at the library hurt?" God help him if Sandy had been harmed. The library being destroyed was bad enough. Jericho already didn't know how to do damage control on this one.

"No. It's Sunday. Only the tow truck driver was killed."

Jericho pinched the spot between his eyes. He didn't even know what day it was anymore. "Okay. Fuck. I need to go talk to Edward. Let's not say anything to him for now. I'm sure he'll hear it from Sandy soon enough, but he doesn't need to know his car destroyed the library. I can't imagine that conversation."

Dante nodded. "Yeah. I agree. We need to find who did this so he's safe. You go distract him. He left his phone in the living room. I'll go stash it in the SUV to buy you some time without Sandy or anyone else calling."

"Good thinking." Jericho hadn't been exaggerating. He appreciated Dante way more than the man could ever know. Nothing felt real any longer, but it helped to be surrounded by people he trusted. He squeezed Dante's shoulder before heading for the stairs. Nothing mattered to him but getting to Edward. How long had a bomb been in Edward's car? What if he had gotten his car started? The thought of losing Edward nearly drove him to his knees. He took the stairs two at a time. Even though their house still wasn't finished, he made sure their bedroom was kept far away from the noise of construction and daily meetings. As Jericho slipped inside their room, his heart slowed. The rage fell away and the fear set in as he spotted Edward sleeping peacefully on their bed. If anything happened to Edward, they would have to take him too. Nothing he accomplished was worth the loss of this wonderful man who had given him a new life. Jericho didn't want anything else for himself. He would walk away from everything with one word from Edward.

Jericho crawled onto the bed and straddled Edward's body. On his stomach, Edward started as Jericho's lips touched his neck. Jericho made a shushing sound against his skin.

"Dante said you came up here to take a nap and I couldn't resist."

"Why did you lie to me about what you do?"

Jericho froze for half a breath. Then he gently turned Edward in his arms. He needed to see Edward's face. "When did I lie to you?"

Edward's expression was half anger and half hurt. Jericho didn't know which way he would land. "You said you were a biohazard specialist when we met. Then when you got this promotion, you said Zander wanted you to take over the east coast."

Jericho nodded. "All of that is true."

Edward stared at him in silence.

A terrible feeling rose in Jericho's gut. "I've never lied to you. Not one time."

"Then why were you interviewing a security team this morning to live with us full time when I didn't even know about it? You never tell me anything. I just live here. Hell, I never even see you anymore. I thought you were setting up a new biohazard cleaning company here on the east coast. I didn't know until Dante told me that's not what you do. I feel like I don't know you at all."

Jericho's eyes fell closed. When they reopened, he found Edward staring at him, looking defeated. He held up one finger and dug out his phone. Jericho pulled up Dante's number. Luckily, he answered on the first ring.

"Hello?"

"Hey, Dante. Unless you get any news about what happened today, I don't want to be disturbed. Please cancel the rest of my appointments for the day."

"Sure thing, boss."

Jericho disconnected the call and set the phone aside. Next, he pulled out his wallet and found his old biohazard certification card. He showed it to Edward. "I promise you; I did crime scene cleanup for Kapra BioRes before the owner, Zander Kapra, asked me to take over as CEO for the Kapra Foundation on the east coast. Basically, he needed me to do what he does in the west but here. I'm a former victim. I've worked for Zander a long time, and I know how the company works. He trusts me and you have no idea how much I regret taking this job already, but here we are." Jericho set his wallet next to his phone. He couldn't look at Edward. "I know you didn't sign up for full-time security and a part-time fiancé. Like I get it if you've got one foot out the door. This isn't what I wanted either."

AVERAGE

"I'm not what you wanted?"

Jericho's gaze shot to Edward. "Of course, you're what I want. You're the only damn thing under this roof I want. If you leave, there'll be nothing left of me. I'll be all Zander's company and nothing else."

Edward's hands ran up Jericho's thighs, massaging. "You're really running a charity that rescues victims of sex trafficking? Wow. That's... wow."

"It's very much a paperwork job... and listening to people's problems." Even Jericho heard the laughter in his voice. He had worked with Zander enough years to know the real heroes were the ones blowing holes in heads at the docks. Jericho was only keeping those people sane and organized.

"These are the same people who rescued you."

It hadn't been a question, but Jericho treated it as one. "In a manner of speaking, yes. I was already an adult when Zander took me in, but I would be dead now if he hadn't. With that said, this organization saves thousands of children every year. As much as I want to walk away, it's so much bigger than me. I've seen too much in my time working for Zander. I went through too much personally to pretend nothing is happening in the world and these kids don't need our help."

"What can I possibly do? I feel like I'm just in the way here. I never get to see you, and even as I'm saying this, I feel like a nag, because you're obviously important and needed. Maybe you're better off without me."

Jericho's throat tightened. "You're not and I'm not." Jericho shifted forward so he could get his hand in his pocket. He pulled out the ring he had placed there earlier. "I've been trying to find the perfect moment to give you this, but there never seems to be a good time."

A line appeared between Edward's eyebrows. "What is it?"

"It's your engagement ring."

He looked taken aback. "Engagement ring? I guess I didn't expect you to get me one."

"Do you still want it?" Jericho held his breath. Edward could walk away and not look back. He could deny Edward the ability to keep him safe and hold him at night. They weren't married yet. Edward didn't owe him shit, and Jericho hadn't done anything to deserve him.

"I love you. Of course, I still want it."

Despite Edward's words, Jericho still didn't feel confident in them. He held out the ring. "I had it custom made for you." The ring was made to look as if it was nothing more than a solid circle of diamonds, but there was enough of a gold band underneath for engraving.

Edward accepted the ring and read the inscription aloud. "*Written in the stars.* Oh my god. This is beautiful." Edward sniffed. "Every time I think I can't love you any more than I already do or that you can't possibly get any better." Edward's expression suddenly fell. "That's part of the problem, I guess. When I thought you lied to me today, I was like, well yeah, that fits. There's the other shoe dropping. Everything has been too perfect. I knew this couldn't be my life. No way could someone amazing love me."

Jericho took the ring from Edward and slipped it on his finger before Edward talked himself out of marrying him. "That's enough of that. I thought we had moved past the bullshit of you not being good enough. Honestly, I don't know what I have to do. Do I need to start spanking you because compliments aren't sinking in the way they should?"

Heat flashed in Edward's eyes.

Jericho's mouth went dry. "I see. Strip."

"It's okay. I shouldn't have doubted you."

It was too late. Jericho hadn't misread what he saw in Edward's eyes. They had met, fallen in love, and moved at lightning speed. In some ways, they were still learning new things about each other. There was nothing sexual Jericho wouldn't do. Nothing. "I didn't ask, Edward. I told you to strip." Jericho moved out of the way so Edward could obey. He stood next to the bed and watched as Edward—with shaky hands—removed his clothes. Jericho kept his features intentionally blank.

The moment Edward was nude, Jericho moved, slowly stripping. He snagged the lube from the bedside table and moved to a nearby chair and sat. "Come here." He stuffed the tube under his thigh so the lube could warm while he tormented Edward.

Edward scrambled from the bed, looking nervous. "I didn't mean to upset you."

Jericho snagged Edward's hips and hauled him forward. It was important Edward understood every aspect of their relationship was a safe space. "I'm not upset with you. It's just long past the time you should've gotten over thinking you're not good enough. That's your mom's voice in your head and it needs to go. Telling you that you're amazing isn't working. Showing you isn't working and apparently even marrying isn't working, so now we'll do this." He pointed at his lap. "Face down."

Edward blushed, but Jericho didn't miss the smile he tried to hide as he did as told. Jericho took a breath as he smoothed his hand over Edward's ass.

He loved Edward's body. It was thick and perfect. He smacked Edward's ass. A barely discernible stifled moan came from Edward. Jericho did it again. This time, harder. Edward gasped. Jericho felt Edward's cock stir against his thigh.

"When I say to you you're the sexiest man I have ever met, I mean that. I need you to own it. Do you understand?"

Edward didn't respond.

Jericho slapped his ass again. "I said, do you understand?"

Edward whimpered.

"That's not an answer."

"Yes."

Jericho opened the lube and coated his fingers. Desire nearly choked him as he spread Edward's cheeks and wet his asshole. "When I tell you I love you and this is forever, what do you say?"

"I love you too, and I know."

"Good boy." Jericho slipped two fingers inside Edward and teased him. "Now, when I say this is the most beautiful body I've ever seen, what do you think?"

Edward didn't respond.

Jericho withdrew his fingers.

Edward whimpered.

Jericho made a tsking sound. "Do you think I'm stupid?"

"Of course not."

Edward's immediate and fierce response gave him hope. Jericho went back to fingering him. "Then why do you treat me like I am? I know what I see when I look at you. I know what I want. Yet you keep treating me like I'm too dumb to know better."

Edward pushed from Jericho's hold and straddled his lap. The fury in his eyes caught Jericho off guard. He had been trying to retrain Edward's thoughts. Instead, it seemed he had pissed him off.

"Don't ever say that to me again. I think you're amazing. In fact, I think there's no one out there who even comes close to comparing to you. When Dante told me what you do today, I was fucking enraged at first. But then, I had some tea and thought things over, and I realized it's really you. I don't know Zander, but fuck if he doesn't know you, because you were made to be the man who's selflessly in charge of this truly ugly thing. Like if there was a single person completely born for this, it's you. You're the purest and most beautiful soul I've ever met. I don't know why I got set in your path that day we collided outside of the bookstore, but goddamn. No one else could love you more than I do. There's nothing I wouldn't stand through with you. So, no. I don't think you're dumb. I just can't stop counting my blessings and hoping like hell I actually deserve them."

Jericho could barely breathe. He had started this game as a fun way to build Edward's confidence. Somehow, Edward had flipped the script and shored him up instead. "I love you." Jericho held Edward's waist and stood. He walked toward the bed. "And as soon as our waiting period ends, I'm marrying you before you get away, because nothing matters more."

Edward sniffed. His eyes filled with tears, taking Jericho by surprise. "Do you really think I think you're stupid?"

Jericho set Edward on the bed and settled between his thighs. "No, baby. I'm sorry I said that. Do we need some counseling or something, because I swear we're not hearing each other?"

Edward shook his head. "I hear you." He sniffed again. "Please make love to me. I feel like I've been slowly losing you."

"That's not possible. I'd give up everything before you."

A tear rolled back into Edward's hair, and Jericho's heart couldn't take it. He shoved Edward's knees up and claimed Edward's mouth as he took Edward's ass. Jericho had to overwhelm Edward. He needed Edward to feel even a quarter of the desperation he felt all hours of the day. Jericho had gone crazy a long time ago. Edward gave him sanity, or at least the only version of it he had ever known. He wouldn't lose him.

Their tongues battled while Jericho rocked inside Edward. Edward pulled Jericho's hair, as if he couldn't get close enough to suit his heart. It was always like this with them. They were like gasoline on an always blazing inferno. There was no way Edward didn't know how horny he made Jericho, because Jericho always came unglued the second they touched. He lost all control. There was desire and then there was whatever the hell this crazy addiction was they shared. Jericho couldn't get enough.

Edward's short fingernails tore at Jericho's back. His moans were like music to Jericho's ears. Jericho pressed his forehead against Edward's chest and stared down the line of their connected bodies and tried to swallow the craziness rising inside him. Someone had tried to kill his baby. He would burn down this whole goddamn world. Nobody harmed this man. Edward thought he was selfless. No. He was just patient. Jericho could sit quietly and wait for his prey to show themselves, but his enemies would lose their heads, nonetheless. He was done playing. Jericho closed his eyes and savored the sensation of the love of his life coming beneath him. As he filled Edward's ass with cum, he vowed everything would change. He would marry Edward ASAP and always put him first. That didn't mean he didn't need to put this town on notice. He was in charge now. It was time for the east coast to meet their kings.

Chapter Eight

EVEN THOUGH EDWARD WOKE alone, he felt more confident than he had in weeks. There was a sense of peace in his soul he had never known. For the first time in his life, Edward knew he was exactly where he was meant to be. He also recognized he had more power than he thought, so that helped. Edward now knew he could find Jericho—wherever he was inside this house—and no matter what he was doing, Edward could plop down in his lap and Jericho's attention would be on him. He understood now. Edward was the most important thing in Jericho's life.

With his faith in life renewed and his nose crammed in his book, Edward headed downstairs. As always, he barely spared his surroundings an ounce of attention. He descended the stairs and flipped the page. Javier was about to learn his longtime lover had been cursed by the gods. Edward had read this one before, but he loved it. He just needed to grab a drink and a snack. Then he would head back to bed to wait for Jericho. He passed a room that was usually empty. The light was on, but that wasn't what caught Edward's eye as he passed. He barely looked up from his book and he questioned if he saw what he thought he had just seen after he went by the open doorway.

AVERAGE

Edward froze.

He retraced his steps and looked inside the room. On a metal folding chair, placed on several layers of thick plastic, sat a bound, bloodied, and bruised old man. He eyed Edward with every bit as much curiosity as Edward eyed him.

"Um. What in the hell is going on here?"

A smile stretched the man's lips. It sent chills down Edward's spine. "Just your garden variety torture session." His gaze moved down Edward's body, making him wish he wore more than just his pajama pants. It was late, and he was in his own home. He hadn't expected to run into anyone. "I swear I can smell his cum on you. It's been a lot of years, but I haven't forgotten how he smells."

The ice in Edward's veins was real. He had never felt so immediately sickened by anyone. Every alarm inside him clanged. Despite the man's expensive—albeit bloodied and torn—suit, if Edward had crossed the man's path on the street, he would've immediately made a wide berth. It was as if evil and perversion dripped from him, even though he looked as normal as the next person.

"Am I supposed to know who you are?" Edward knew he should have moved along and pretended ignorance, the way he did to all Jericho's business. This one time, he couldn't. Something kept his feet glued to the floor. There was something about the way this man looked at him.

"Possibly." Edward wasn't fooled by the casual tone. He wanted Edward to stay.

He wanted his words to hurt. "I know you, though."

"Hmm. Okay." Edward turned to go. He would pretend he hadn't seen this. It was for the best.

"I tried to kill you, but I was sloppy. Instead, I only ended up blowing up your car, a tow truck driver, and half the public library."

That drew Edward up short. "Come again?"

A low, evil-sounding chuckle fell from his cut lips. His dead-looking brown eyes crinkled in the corners despite one being nearly swelled closed. "I'd love to. Unfortunately, there's no time machine that'll make my beautiful Jericho ten again. That was my favorite age with him. He was perfect. You should have seen him. He was so small."

The man's head snapped back before Edward realized his fingers had tightened on the hardback book he held. He swung with zero memory of doing so. The second time was on purpose when the first hit didn't bring him enough satisfaction. Oddly, neither did the third blow. Before the fourth blow landed, the book disappeared from his hand and a strong arm encircled his waist. He was lifted from his feet.

Jericho's lips touched his ear as he carried Edward from the room. "Shh. It's okay. Let it go, baby. He's done."

Edward fought to catch his breath. Rage and hatred completely owned him. He fought to get back to finish the job. Edward couldn't believe the man who harmed his angel was under their roof and still breathed. He didn't deserve to have oxygen.

Jericho tossed Edward over his shoulder and headed outside. The cool air touched his skin, clearing his mind. A wave of helplessness and sadness washed over him. He wanted to protect his baby and fix the past. Edward wanted to do something. Anything. He couldn't do anything. Helpless tears gathered in his eyes. Jericho kept moving until he found a spot where they were alone in the darkness. He sat on the ground beneath a tree with Edward in his lap and held him.

With his lips pressed to Edward's temple, Jericho kissed Edward and shushed him. "It's okay. You can let it go. It's all right."

Tears streamed down Edward's face. He was enraged and hurt on Jericho's behalf. For the first time in his life, he wanted to kill someone, and he had no qualms about it. There was no guilt. He wanted that man dead. "Why are you so calm? This is not okay. Why is that monster in our home?"

Jericho rubbed his back. "Dante arranged for a towing company to pick up your car. When they tried to move it, it exploded. After looking into it, we found out the man who once owned me was behind planting the bomb. I didn't even know he was still alive until tonight."

Edward's shoulders fell. He collapsed into Jericho's hold. Until that moment, he hadn't wanted to be honest with himself. He had known. Edward wasn't an idiot. He had known all of this. Until he had seen it with his eyes and felt the murder in his veins, he hadn't fully understood why he had turned a blind eye and played dumb. Now he wished he could go back and un-hear the terrible things that monster had said. Edward could never, ever unlearn this moment.

"I want him dead." No one could have been more shocked by the venom in Edward's voice than Edward. He didn't care. That snake had to die.

Jericho's arms tightened around Edward. "What did he say to you?"

Edward fought the urge to hiss. "It doesn't matter. He doesn't deserve to live."

"I don't disagree."

Jericho sounded so calm, and Edward didn't understand. That gross, vile thing had tortured Jericho for years. Yet Jericho calmly held Edward and tried keeping him calm. "How are you not in there tearing out his eyes?"

To Edward's surprise, a smile touched Jericho's lips. "Because I have you. I won. Any second now, he'll be dead, and in his last moments of life, he'll know that not only is it because of me, but also, I'm living my best life completely unbothered by the loss of his. All because I have you. Not this job or this house. Just you. I was born to be used and die, but that's not what happened. I ended up becoming the happiest man in the world, and that's all because of you."

Edward fell forward and pressed his forehead to Jericho's. With his eyes closed, he breathed Jericho's air and let his existence soothe him. He was still furious. Edward still wanted to murder someone, but this was more important.

"Can we just fucking get married already?"

A laugh burst from Jericho at Edward's question. "Absolutely. It's about goddamn time, honestly." Jericho stood so fast Edward didn't completely understand how he found himself back inside the house. Jericho barked orders at Dante and a few men Edward had never seen, while Edward quietly clung to Jericho's side. In a matter of minutes, in his half-finished kitchen, a sleep-mussed judge ambled in and asked them both to sign some papers.

His dark gaze landed on Edward. He handed Edward a ring. "Do you take Jericho Wrath to be your lawfully wedded husband from now until your dying breath?"

Edward didn't think. He simply answered the completely emotionless question. "I do."

The judge nodded. "Good. Put the ring on him." Edward chuckled but did as told.

Their grumpy officiator handed Jericho a ring. "Do you take Edward Jones to be your lawfully wedded husband from now until your dying breath?"

Jericho held Edward's stare, looking solemn and steady. "I do."

"Good. Put the ring on him. I now pronounce you husbands for life. You may kiss and now I'd like to return to bed. Have a nice evening."

With a laugh, Edward threw himself into Jericho's arms. He didn't know how Jericho had convinced the judge to leave his bed, and get there so fast, to come marry them, but he was happier than he had ever been. Their lips met and nothing else mattered. Edward already knew he would love this man for the rest of his life. Everything would be perfect.

The level of shock Jericho felt upon seeing Edward beating William with a book was only eclipsed by his own reaction. After two hours of torturing the man who had held him prisoner for most of his life, Jericho had needed a break. When he had returned to find Edward taking over the job for him, he had been more than a little turned on by this new side of Edward. Jericho didn't doubt, if he hadn't intervened, Edward would have killed him. Part of him wondered if he should have let him. Maybe—despite Jericho being the victim—it was Edward's right, as his husband, to end William. After all, Jericho would feel it was his if anyone harmed Edward. Either way, he was proud as hell to be Edward's husband. There was no one else out there who compared.

The weight of his wedding ring felt perfect on his finger. When he came up for air, Edward looked dazed from their kiss. Happiness roared through Jericho. He had never been this lucky. Dante smiled like an idiot nearby, and a hint of guilt hit him. There was a man waiting at home for Dante too and the whole bullshit with William had kept Dante there for way too long.

"You should go home."

Dante's smile never wavered. "Marshall will understand this one time. Congratulations, guys! I'm so happy for you two."

Edward blushed. "Thank you. Jericho is right, though. You should go home. Marshall won't want you working here anymore if we keep you like this all the time. It's not fair to you. I promise we'll find a way to make it up to you."

Dante made a dismissive motion. "I don't know if you know this, but Jericho is like family to me. I'm glad I got to be here for this. You two should definitely pack a bag, though, and get out of here.

Gas up the jet and take a honeymoon. You deserve it."

Edward's gaze flickered toward the hall. Jericho knew his thoughts had already turned toward their unsavory guest. Edward focused on Dante again. "That bastard ruined my favorite book."

Dante tried and failed to hide a smile. "That is something we cannot tolerate, Mr. Wrath. Would you like to shoot him, or should I?"

"I'll decide when we get there."

Jericho bit the inside of his cheek to keep from laughing as Dante handed Edward a gun. "That is your right, sir."

Jericho stopped him before he made it three steps. "Baby, you have to live with whatever you decide."

Gorgeous brown eyes looked at him with an unexpected innocence and a clear conscience. "That's not a fear I have."

Jericho nodded and let Edward go. He didn't go with him. He let Dante accompany Edward because Jericho wouldn't give William the satisfaction of seeing him as he died. Instead, he headed for the bedroom and dragged their luggage from the closet.

Edward returned as if nothing happened, and—really—it might as well have. William was nothing. He was the trash being taken out. Jericho didn't even want to know who pulled the trigger. As far as he was concerned, William had died decades ago. He found the black and red t-shirt of Edward's he loved and packed it.

"Where are we headed anyhow? I've never really been anywhere."

Jericho met Edward's stare. It hit him anew they were married. A smile lit his face. "I don't know. Anywhere at all is fine with me, as long as we're together. Where have you always wanted to go?"

Edward looked thoughtful for a moment before a bright smile lit his face. "It's going to seem silly to you, most likely, but I've never been to Vegas. I know it's this big tourist spot that's not very quiet or romantic, but I've always wanted to go."

Jericho shrugged. "It's like I said, if I'm with you, we can go wherever you like. There are aspects to Vegas that can be romantic. At least, I'm a firm believer we can make any place a passionate retreat, if we try hard enough."

For a moment, they stared at each other, wearing matching smiles. Then Edward unexpectedly squealed in delight. "I can't believe we're married and we're going to Vegas. You're really my husband now."

"I really am."

Edward launched himself at Jericho and kissed every place he could reach. Their laughter turned breathless as their kisses became heated.

"You need to change."

"I know," Edward said as he changed angles and nipped at Jericho's neck. His hand—somehow—found its way inside Jericho's pants.

"Fuck. How do you always make me so hot, so fast? Someone is probably already waiting to race us out of here and to the airport."

"Probably." Edward didn't sound concerned.

Jericho wasn't either. He held Edward and let Edward stroke him into blinding oblivion. By tomorrow, they would be in Vegas. He would show Edward everything he had missed over the years. It was the perfect place to visit for someone who had been nowhere. Vegas was like seeing a miniature version of the rest of the world. From there, Edward could decide which parts of the world he wanted to see more of, and Jericho would give him his wish. Maybe this wasn't exactly the average life he pictured when he collided with Edward outside the bookstore that first day. But this was their version of normal and it was perfect. It was beautiful. Jericho wouldn't want life to be any other way.

Chapter Nine

FIFTY. DAMN. WHERE HAD the years gone? How had Zander turned fifty when he wasn't looking? His gaze moved across the room at the smiling, laughing, and dancing men scattered around his ballroom. Some talked. Others drank. No one looked unhappy. He wasn't vain enough to think he had done that, but wow. Zander really hoped he had played some small part in healing the people who joined him to celebrate tonight. Reality slapped him so hard, he lost his breath. He was celebrating his birthday. Zander had really let his sneaky-ass husband plan this party without a qualm, knowing damn well he didn't celebrate this day. Yet, he had let the past go at some point without even realizing it. He was the person who had done the most healing in the room. Zander owed the most to the people surrounding him.

His gaze found his husband. Zander drew a slow breath. Twelve of the greatest years on this planet had been with his dark-haired god. Honey-colored eyes turned his way. A smirk touched Maverick's lips. Butterflies stirred in Zander's stomach as if it was the first time, he saw the man who had completely stolen him. No one else existed for him. Maverick winked and went back to entertaining their guests. Zander fought the urge to demand everyone leave right then. Maverick had worked too hard on this party. Zander forced himself to behave. Still, the crowd was getting to be a bit much. He cast a quick glance to make sure no one watched and then he slipped down the hallway. It was his house. He could do what he wanted. Go where he wanted.

With his hands shoved in his pockets, Zander meandered down the hall. As the music and voices got smaller and the sound of rushing water got louder, Zander's peace returned. Even though he built his indoor training areas for just that purpose—training—its rock face and waterfalls were also a peaceful place to sit when he felt overwhelmed, which felt like always these last couple of years. Things had gotten better with Jericho's help. He hoped that would only improve as more and more people turned to Jericho over him. After all, Zander wasn't getting any younger. He spotted Bear and Creed hanging out in the shadows near the waterfall. Even though they stole a few kisses, he knew they were keeping an eye on their bosses. He had worked with Bear enough times to know Bear would die for the people he loved. Jericho was impossible not to adore.

"I'm convinced you could climb it."

"I absolutely could not, but that's flattering."

Zander's gaze moved away from Bear and Creed and shot toward the laughter and voices. A smile snapped to his lips. Jericho pawed his husband while Edward eyed the climbing wall. He pointed at the lowest foothold. "Yes. See. The very first step. That's where I would die."

"You would not. I watched you dodge construction workers for almost a year while your nose was stuck in a book. That takes talent. You're way more graceful than you give yourself credit for being."

"Hmm. Well. Let's not find out."

Zander chuckled. "It's the trip down you have to worry about."

The pair turned. They wore matching smiles.

"Hey." Jericho rushed forward and hugged Zander. "Happy birthday. You've been so bombarded by people tonight, I haven't gotten a chance to talk to you." He motioned Edward's way. "This is my husband."

"Edward. Yes. We've met," Zander said, stepping forward and shaking a visibly confused-looking Edward's hand. "Hello, Edward. We meet again. It's good to see you."

"Oh my god. You're Zander? I mean, obviously, you're Zander, but you're *the* Zander. I'm so confused right now."

Jericho's gaze moved between them. "Wait. What?"

Zander winced. "I met Edward at a poetry reading while in Cage Beach some time back."

Edward nodded. "It was almost two years ago. We had a very philosophical discussion about a poem that was read. He swears it was about love. I still say it was about murder."

Zander tossed a laughing look Jericho's way. "So we asked the poet and he confirmed it was about both."

Jericho's expression changed and Zander knew the puzzle pieces were starting to click together in his head.

Edward motioned Zander's way. "In fact, Zander is the reason I bumped into you that day you saw me at the bookstore. That was the day of the poetry reading. He bumped me from behind and then I bumped into you."

Jericho's eyebrows rose and Zander knew he was caught. "Is that so?"

Zander shrugged. "The place was slammed. It might've happened like that. I'm surprised you didn't see me there."

Jericho bit his bottom lip and shook his head. "Maybe I would have if I hadn't caught sight of an angel and decided to follow him to the tea shop instead."

"Lucky break, that," Zander said, trying not to gloat too hard.

"Mhmm, yes. Lucky break." The laughter in Jericho's voice couldn't be missed.

"Anyhow," Zander said, looking between the happy couple. "Marriage suits you both. You look happy."

"We are." The way they answered at the same time said a lot. Zander didn't need to regret meddling. Plus, he honestly hadn't done much. He had known Jericho long enough to know his type. Intelligence was his weakness. Edward was smart and gorgeous. He would keep Jericho on his toes. Zander had just forced Edward into Jericho's path. Jericho had been the one who had fallen—like the smart man Zander knew him to be.

"There you are. This is supposed to be your party."

At Maverick's appearance, Jericho flashed him a sympathetic smile and tossed an arm over Edward's shoulders. "Come on, gorgeous. Let me show you where my old bedroom used to be."

Zander chuckled. "We keep it at the ready for your visits."

Jericho winked and steered Edward down the hall, leaving Zander to deal with the consequences of sneaking away from his party.

Maverick eyed him. His expression didn't give anything away. "Are you angry I threw you a surprise party?"

That was the last thing Zander expected. "No. You know whatever makes you happy makes me happy."

Maverick visibly drew a steady breath. "It's your birthday. It's not supposed to be about making me happy."

Maverick knew why Zander didn't celebrate his birthday, but he tried every year for Maverick's sake. Plus, he knew fifty was supposed to be a big deal or whatever. "You're amazing. The way you continuously go way too far for me doesn't go unnoticed. I couldn't love or appreciate you more."

"But…"

Zander's eyebrows snapped together. "There's no but. I knew if I stepped away from the party you would follow, and I would have you to myself."

Maverick snorted. His eyes flashed with humor. He shuffled closer, crowding Zander's space. They matched each other in size. Zander's skin heated at the wicked glint in Maverick's eyes. "Well, here I am. You got your wish. What now?"

Everything else disappeared. Zander's gaze dropped to Maverick's lips. He swore the room heated. In a flash, Maverick snagged his throat and hauled him closer. A satisfied laugh burst from Zander. He knew how to torment Maverick without saying a word.

"Fucking tease. Stop playing with me and kiss me."

At Maverick's demand and beneath his controlling touch, Zander opened as Maverick's mouth covered his. Zander took a deep breath. Love filled him.

AVERAGE

Maverick was the realest reason Zander needed to save as many people as possible. He needed to know he deserved this because how could anyone? Their love was so big. It was so powerful and all consuming. Until Zander met Maverick, he hadn't known anything this beautiful existed. He couldn't stop earning the beautiful life Maverick gave him.

Maverick's strong arms encircled him and held him tighter as his kisses turned hotter by the second. Zander handed himself over to the man who owned him. Wherever Maverick led, Zander would go. They could go back to the party or straight to bed. Either way, Zander was onboard. Just as Maverick had been at his side through every crazy decision Zander had made over the years, Zander would always be at Maverick's side. Zander would keep trying to save the world. Maverick would keep trying to save him. It was the perfect marriage. The perfect life. He only hoped he gave people even half what he gained with his freedom. After all, everyone deserved a happy ending like his.

Please consider leaving a review at the retailer where you purchased this book. Reviews really help with a book's visibility, which allows me to continue writing more stories. Thank you, Charity.

About the Author

About the Author

Charity Parkerson is an award-winning and multi-published author with several companies. Born with no filter from her brain to her mouth, she decided to take this odd quirk and insert it in her characters.

*Eight-time Readers' Favorite Award Winner

CHARITY PARKERSON

*2015 Passionate Plume Award Finalist
*2013 Reviewers' Choice Award Winner
*2012 ARRA Finalist for Favorite Paranormal Romance
*Five-time winner of The Mistress of the Darkpath

Connect with her online:

*Sign up for her newsletter: https://sendfox.com/charityparkerson
*Join her readers' group on Facebook: http://bit.ly/CharitysTribe
*Website: https://www.charityparkerson.com
*A list of her social media accounts and giveaways all in one place: http://hy.page/charityparkerson

Content

CONTENT WARNING: THIS SERIES is darker than my usual writing. Since these books bring back Zander and his fight against child trafficking, the deal in kidnapping, sex trafficking (along with everything entailed in that), suicide, and murder. A lot of these characters survived the worst things imaginable and now live with the scars. But now they fight to save people like them.